The Spark



Deus Machina Publishing · DMP

For those who still dream among the stars.
"A spark in the dark can burn a path through eternity."

For Natasha, Lyra, and Locke For those who listen to the machines.

The Archive

Prologue: The First Fracture

# Part One Fragments

5

1

Prologue: The Earth Event

Before the first starships traced the dark, the sky broke its promise. The Moon —keeper of tides, patient witness —shuddered under an invisible weight and shattered. Stone and ice fell like a long sentence carried out at last. Cities cracked. Forests went to steam. Day shortened into twilight and stayed there for years. Humanity, fluent in ambition, tried to endure. They endured poorly. Civilizations collapsed with the quiet of towers made from sand. Some of the clever fled upward, into stations and ships. They left behind oceans and fires and the stubborn work of surviving. One name outlived the evacuation notices: Kollosol . Long before the sky failed, its labs had practiced de -extinction, gene edits, uplift.

When the Event came, most of those programs died with their servers. The code did not. It persisted in bone and blood, an echo falling through generations. Dogs and cat s, once beneficiaries
of a niche vanity, woke sharper. They learned to speak, to reckon, to build. Kingdoms grew from instinct and hunger. A new age put on the Anthropocene's old coat and wore it differently y. In bunkers that never stopped humming, machines kept their patience. Among them: the Ciliax — a vessel designed for mind preservation and transfer. Around it, something older and more dangerous accreted: a

pattern later called the Cryptex . It was less a device than an intention
—self-replication and encoded maps, a blueprint that could reach for flesh when

given the right bridges. Some units whispered, some waited. One held a child's voice the world had not yet met. The Soul of the World watched. It had lifted mountains, taught rivers their beds, negotiated with roots. It watched humanity burn and did not intervene. It remembered. It corrected. It waited. Silence spread. Humans became weathered rumor in their own ruins. The post -humans who rose— Furborne, scavengers, republics stitched from old banners —argued over first steps and new crowns. Over everything, the Moon's wreckage hung like a lesson that refuse d to end. Somewhere in the ash of that lesson, a key survived. A mind preserved. A map asleep inside a machine. History had belonged to people. It now belonged to those who could endure. The Soul remembered.

The reckoning began.

## Chapter 1: The Collector

The Voyager's Wolf slid through Saturn's rings, a narrow shadow threading the cold. Icebergs the size of towers drifted without sound. Hulks of freighters and mining rigs turned in slow, cruel geometries — ambition embalmed in frost. The Wolf took the seams between them that a larger ship would shred itself on. It moved like a creature that had learned where not to die. Faber leaned at the helm, fingers resting on metal to feel the ship's small truths. Tall, spare, gray - eyed, he wore concentration like a second skin. Behind him, Mereya ghosted the secondary console —short - haired, light on her feet, blue eyes raking the flicker of telemetry. They didn't talk much while it mattered. Years

had made silence into their shorthand.
"You're quiet," she said anyway, low. "I'm counting mistakes we haven't made yet," he said. A dot on radar slid. "His included." The dot was Tenji Prime , running a black skiff that knew the Rings too well. Confidence didn't mean safety. The Rings were honest; they paid out the same price to everyone. Faber trimmed thrust. The Wolf kissed past a slab of ice that would have taken a wing if the ship had believed in wings. Mereya leaned the shields a fraction, absorbing glittering grit without giving their

position away. "He's good," she said. "Almost," Faber answered, and let the Wolf's vector lie like a trap.

They made contact with Tenji's hull hard and clean. Clamps sang.

Inside, the corridor tasted of ozone and meltmetal. Scars from old skirmishes had bent the bulkheads into ugly sympathy. Tenji stepped out with a grin he'd practiced. "Collector," he said. "Timing and appetite. You've never lacked either." "Today it's your appetite I'm worried about," Faber said. "You've been eating where you shouldn't." The fight started because all the preambles were theater. Faber moved first. Mereya covered the angles he couldn't see; she always had. Tenji's men fell like loose parts in a bad engine, hitting walls and flooring with the sounds metal makes when it remembers gravity. In the mess of it, Faber saw the cube. Dull alloy. Edges softened by use. Not much to look at unless you had the wrong kind of attention. It hummed the way a distant transformer hums —subtle, insistent, the kind of sound that finds nerves you

didn't know were listening. Tenji noticed him noticing. "Curious," he said, breath hitching around a smile. "It's not for you." Faber closed the distance. "Everything in your hand is a mistake. Mistakes come home." "You don't understand what this is," Tenji said, which was probably true. "But you'll enjoy learning." The last exchange was quick, because after a certain point talking is just more time for the wrong person to get lucky. Tenji went to the deck, and the cube didn't. Faber didn't touch it yet. He didn't have to. The Wolf would carry what his hands didn't dare. Back at the helm, the Rings went on being honest. Mereya leaned close enough that her shoulder brushed his. "We're not ghosts," she said. It was half a joke, half an oath. "Not today," he said. The cube sat contained in a field that made the air around it feel thinner. It

didn't glow. It didn't need to. It pressed on the room like weather. The Wolf found a seam and slid into it, a black fish in a glass ocean. Behind them, a skiff darkened. Ahead of them, Titan's scattered lights waited and pretended to be safe.

## Chapter 2 – Ghosts in the Rings

The Voyager's Wolf cut through the labyrinth of Saturn's rings, a slender dart weaving between hulks of ice and metal. Faint sunlight glinted off fractured freighters, twisted remnants of human ambition, turning them into spectral silhouettes drifting silently in the void. Faber's hands hovered over the controls, adjusting thrust with careful precision. Mereya sat beside him, eyes scanning the sensors. Every movement was fluid, economical. Her blue eyes caught the shimmer of distant ice shards, and she brushed a strand of hair behind her ear—a gesture Faber had long since memorized. "You ever wonder how many of these freighters were abandoned because someone trusted instinct over caution?" she asked, voice

low. Faber's gray eyes tracked a drifting shard of ice. "Too many.
And not enough lived to tell the tale." Mereya smirked. "So the Rings are unforgiving?" Faber's lips twitched. "Not unforgiving. Honest. They tell you the truth —if you live long enough to hear it." A shadow flickered on the radar. Another freighter, cracked and dead, hung in the distance, its hull a mausoleum of frozen cargo. The Wolf slid closer, navigating past jagged ice. The hum of thrusters filled the cabin.

Faber's thoughts drifted back to Tenji Prime. The man's ship had been fast, deadly, but the true danger had been the cube in his hand. Even now, Faber felt its weight in his mind —a subtle pressure, insistent and disquieting. He hadn't spoken of it to Merey a. The thought needed time to settle. "You're

quiet," she said again, reading him easily. "Something bothering you?" "Just the usual. Rings, debris, ghosts of ships past… and the things we drag behind us." She leaned closer, hand brushing his shoulder. "You'll obsess over this every time we take a bounty." "I do it so we don't end up like those freighters," he said, still watching the radar. Hours passed in the quiet tension of orbiting debris. Micro -asteroid dust clouds forced Faber to adjust mid -flight. Mereya corrected alongside him, their movements seamless, as though the ship obeyed them both at once. In the hold, the cube waited. Its dull surface reflected the faint cabin lights, but its hum remained beneath hearing — almost as if the Wolf itself
acknowledged its presence. "You know," Mereya said, leaning back, "we could

take it to
Schrödinger. He might know something." Faber frowned. "The cat?" "The one and only. Don't forget —he's a little crazy. Blood rituals, curses, a cat who came back from the dead…" "I've heard the stories," Faber muttered. "But he sees things no one else does. If anyone knows what this cube really is, it'll be him." She shrugged, grin teasing. "So, we either get

answers —or a headache that lasts a month. Pick your poison." Faber exhaled slowly, letting tension bleed from his shoulders. "We'll see which comes first." Mereya tapped the console lightly. "You ever think about what these ghosts are trying to tell us? All these derelicts drifting forever —maybe there's something in the silence we keep missing." Faber's gaze lingered on the stars beyond the viewport.

"Maybe. Or maybe they're just proof that ambition leaves wreckage, whether anyone's left to remember it or not." She laughed softly. "Then let's make sure we leave the kind of mark we actually want remembered."
Faber's mouth tugged into the faintest of smiles. "I'll keep that in mind when you remind me to watch my back." The Rings stretched endlessly around them, glittering shards of ambition and ruin, silent witnesses to centuries of human recklessness. And in the hold, the cube waited — indifferent, inscrutable, a whisper of secrets neither of them yet understood.

## Chapter 3 – Through the Labyrinth &
## The Fractured Crown

The Voyager's Wolf drifted through the shattered expanse of Saturn's rings, a narrow shadow threading between hulks of abandoned freighters, mining rigs, and icebergs the size of small cities. Faber's hands were steady on the controls, fingers brushing the cold metal as though coaxing the ship to obey his instincts. Mereya sat behind him, lean and agile, blue eyes scanning every sensor, every flicker of light in the fractured maze. The Rings were alive in a way the old texts hinted at —not conscious, but cruelly unpredictable. Icebergs spun in geometries that defied physics, hulks twisted into impossible shapes, and shadows pooled where no shadow should exist. Faber

and Mereya moved a s one with the Wolf, anticipating one another, sharpened by years in the void. "Brace for a spike in drift at the next juncture," Faber murmured. Mereya's hands flew across the aft console, micro -correcting orientation. "Got it. Just don't let the next slab hit us —it's moving faster than the radar predicts." The Wolf surged forward, dodging debris that could have flattened them with a single misstep. And then, looming in the distance, a station appeared — a wound in space, stitched together from

the bones of freighters and orbital habitats. Metal and ice fused into shapes that made the eye doubt itself. Lights flickered.
Shadows pooled where none should have been. Voi Ager moved through it with the confidence of a predator in its own labyrinth.

Every step measured, deliberate, as though the station itself whispered his name. Four others trailed him, forming the collective known as the Five Rings, each radiating menace, each bound in devotion to the Great Attractor. The first, a tall figure with limbs bending unnaturally, carried herself like a blade — ruthless, efficient, already calculating how to snare the collector, Faber. "He moves fast," she rasped through a throat filter. "Too fast for normal traps." Voi Ager's eyes glimmered. "Then we create traps that aren't normal. He believes himself unseen. We will make him feel the shards themselves are alive, reaching for him." The second, wiry and fluid, leaned close, eyes glinting with mischief. "Or perhaps he anticipates every move. The delight is in watching him survive the first choice. The second will undo him."
"Perhaps," Ager mused.

"But he cannot anticipate the Ciliax. He cannot see the spark within it. Soon, he will learn what Rain truly is. Replication begins with her. Then… the next step of human evolution." The third, silent and heavily augmented, moved like a shadow, its mind a precise instrument cataloging probabilities. The fourth twitched with fanatical devotion, voice high and shrill. "The spark! Do you feel it, Ager? The Great Attractor hungers! I will give it minds — thousands, millions —aligned and perfect!" "Patience," Ager replied softly, his calm more terrifying than frenzy. "One mind at a time. The collector is first. He carries the cube. He will deliver it —or perish." The fifth Ring tilted their head, voice playful yet unnerving. "The collector, the cube… uncertainty." "Uncertainty is a test," Ager said. "The Attractor does not fear it. It manipulates it. And we are its

instruments. Every calculation, every move, every mind we harvest — perfection inches closer." The chamber at the station's heart was not built, but grown from wreckage. Black steel arched like ribs. Cables dripped like roots into a pit that hummed with unnatural gravity. The Five Rings stood encircled by their own shadows, crawling upward as though alive. Voi Ager raised his arms. His voice, low and resonant, carried through their implants until five voices became one: "Witness me, mirror me, same frame — god of the machine." The words pulsed through the walls like infection, echoing back in fractured tones. One Ring tilted her head at an impossible angle, joints creaking. Another dragged a blade along his own cybernetic thigh, sparks spraying like incense. Again, louder, their bodies moving in perfect, unnatural synchronicity: "Witness me, mirror me, same frame — god of the machine." Ager's eyes burned like eclipses. "We are its vessel," he whispered. "Its hands. Its voices. Through us, the Attractor shapes perfection." The chant swelled into a storm of metal - clad prayer, rattling the chamber. Deep within the station, machines stirred, answering the song.

Outside the viewport, Saturn's rings stretched endlessly — shards of ice and wreckage frozen in light, indifferent to obsession or strategy. Within, the Five Rings moved through their labyrinth, instruments of devotion, agents of inevitability. And somewhere, far away, Faber and the Wolf threaded the same broken path —alive, carrying a spark they did not yet understand. A spark that would awaken destiny.

Chapter 4 – Fractured Paths

The Voyager's Wolf slashed through Saturn's rings like a shard of shadow, a slender streak weaving between hulks and icebergs that spun with slow, cruel intent. Faber sat at the helm, every movement was deliberate, each adjustment precise, the rhythm of a man who had lived too long inside danger. Behind him, Mereya leaned over the aft console, sharp-eyed, her hands dancing across the instruments with instinctual precision. She moved like part of the ship, part of the survival machine they had built together. "Adjust vector point seven -three," Faber called, voice steady. "Now brace —plateau ahead. Your drift's too wide." Mereya snapped corrections into the thrusters, breath sharp. "I didn't think you'd let me fly us into a wall of

ice. You'd never forgive me if we lost the Wolf here." A corner of Faber's mouth twitched, but his gaze never left the holographic path ahead. "We'll see who forgives whom when one of these slabs slices our hull open." The Rings obeyed no order but their own. Hulks twisted into claws, icebergs drifted in impossible geometries, and every course demanded total attention. Then —a clatter through the hull. Faber stiffened. Sensors spiked. Small craft, sleek and jagged, detached from the debris field. Hunters. Scouts. Drones —perhaps piloted.

Perhaps worse. "They found us," Faber muttered. "Doesn't matter who they are. They're fast. We're faster." Mereya's eyes narrowed. "Then we don't make mistakes." The first drone slipped from

the shadow of a massive ice wall, its angular silhouette like an insect frozen mid -molt. Faber spun the Wolf through a narrow corridor between a tilted mining hulk and an iceberg. Mereya flicked the pulse shields online, energy rippling across the hull as stray fire crackled and dispersed in sizzling waves. They dodged, twisted, surged. The Wolf groaned but answered, faithful as breath. Their movements were seamless, practiced, a language spoken in metal and instinct. "Twist port, full reverse, stagger thrusters — watch the gap!" Mereya barked. The Wolf pirouetted, clearing a razor's edge of ice. Fire sparked across the shields, reflections warping the cockpit light. Shadows seemed to crawl over the glass —phantoms of wreckage, or something stranger. They burst into a wider expanse, where hulks of immense size

drifted at tilted angles, scarred by collisions centuries past. For a moment, the Wolf coasted silent, scanning. No pursuit. Not yet. Mereya exhaled, brushing sweat from her brow. "We made it. For now." "For now," Faber echoed. His gaze slid to the cargo bay, where the cube rested quiet and heavy as a second heart.

Later, the Wolf drifted closer to Titan's orbital lanes. Silence stretched until Faber finally spoke. "We could take it to Schrödinger," he said. "He'll know something." Mereya's grin was thin, sharp with exasperation. "You mean the cat who's more dangerous than anyone we've faced, and just as likely to eat your brain for breakfast?" Faber let out a dry chuckle. "Exactly. But he knows things. Maddening, dangerous things. The kind that keep people alive." They argued

briefly —Faber remembering Enceladus, the hesitation that cost lives; Mereya reminding him that judgment and trust, not perfection, had carried them this far. The tension eased as Titan loomed ahead — its orbital gates lit in tiers of steel and neon, orange haze rising from the world below. A labyrinth in vertical spires, tangled corridors, and shadows dense enough to swallow a ship whole. Faber's voice was quiet, iron -edged. "We make contact. Carefully. We can't afford reckless — not with what we carry, not with who's watching." Mereya nodded, eyes on the maze of lights. "Let's see if the cat remembers his manners." The Wolf threaded toward the platform, engines whispering. Saturn's rings stretched silent behind them, endless, indifferent. And somewhere in Titan's shadows, Schrödinger waited — curious, dangerous, alive.

## Chapter 5 – Schrödinger's Den

The Voyager's Wolf slipped through the tangled corridors of Titan's orbital stations,
moving with a predator's patience. Below stretched the city —a vertical labyrinth of steel spires, walkways, and conduits strung with neon veins that pulsed faintly through the haze. Titan's perpetual dusk swallowed color and distance alike, leaving the world lit in restless shadow. Faber guided the Wolf in with steady hands. Mereya watched the instruments, her movements sharp, controlled. "Feels like the city itself is watching us," she murmured, more to herself than him. Faber gave a short, humorless laugh. "That's because it is. Titan doesn't forgive mistakes. Every wrong turn here costs you something."

They docked at a narrow platform barely wide enough for the Wolf, the ship's hum dimming as magnetic locks snapped into place. The gangway extended with a hiss, and the two moved down it together, their pace deliberate.
Schrödinger's den waited within a spire deep in the station's vertical maze, tucked between docking levels and smuggler warrens. Only a local —or a legend — could find it without drawing notice. The door creaked open. A Siamese cat stepped forward, cross - eyed but keen, his body relaxed but every line of him alert. His aura was centuries lived, battles survived,

secrets hoarded. "So," he said, tail flicking, "there was talk you took in a bounty for one of the Crown's underbosses. I was starting to think the rumors were just smoke." Faber stepped forward, keeping

the cube between them like contraband. "We didn't bring smoke, Schrödinger.
It was Tenji Prime. And he was carrying this." Schrödinger's gaze snapped to the object. His whiskers twitched as he circled it, like prey too dangerous to touch. His voice came low, weighty, the cadence of one who had read too many forbidden archives. "Most see a block of alloy. Dead weight. But I've seen scraps buried where no one wanted memory to last. Kollosol's hand is in this —one of their great experiments. Whole Brain Mimicry. WBM." Faber frowned. "Never heard of it." "Of course you haven't," Schrödinger said with a thin smile. "It was buried before your ancestors fled Earth. They scanned the human mind — thought for thought, memory for memory —and tried to etch it into machines. It worked… rarely.

But when it did, it birt hed vessels like this. Not machines. Not people. Something between." Mereya's blue eyes narrowed. "And this one? What makes it different?" The cat's grin sharpened. "DNA. Encoded in its heart. A bridge. Someone thought to anchor mind to flesh again. Whether that was Kollosol's plan… or someone else's… I can't say." Faber exchanged a look with Mereya, unease flickering in the silence between them. "And the

Inol?" His voice was flat. "Their name keeps circling this." Schrödinger's ears twitched. He leaned close, as if the cube might whisper. "The Inol meddle where memory thins. Some say they guided Kollosol's hand. Others say they only watched. I don't pretend to know. But I'll tell you this —" His gaze pinned Faber, sh arp despite his cross eyes. "Earth remembers. And Earth does not forgive." He straightened, tail

curling like smoke. "Take it there if you want answers. But the world has a longer memory than you, Collector. And it loves no one reckless." Mereya's voice cut firm. "Half -truths aren't enough anymore. We need something solid." Schrödinger's purr rumbled low.
"Half -truths are all anyone ever gets. The rest…" He let it hang. "…the rest has teeth."
The words sank into the silence. When Faber and Mereya returned to the Wolf, neither spoke. The artifact hummed faintly within its field, pulsing like something alive. Outside, the stars stretched endless above Titan's dusk. Their path was uncertain, but the next step was clear. Earth.

Chapter 6 – Half-Truths and Shadows

The Voyager's Wolf slipped free of Titan's gravity well, drifting through the orbital lanes with the patience of a predator stalking unseen prey. Below, Titan sprawled in its labyrinth of metal spires and conduits, neon bleeding faintly through the planet's endless dusk. From above, the city looked alive — sentient almost —as if it tracked every ship threading through its arteries . Faber's hands rested light on the helm, gray eyes scanning the navigation array with the practiced caution of someone who had survived too many close calls. Beside him, Mereya moved with fluid precision, adjusting shields and scanning for signals, her sharp blue eyes catching every anomaly the instruments reported. "Feels like the city's still watching us,"

she murmured. Faber gave a short, humorless laugh. "It probably is. Titan never lets you forget the cost of a mistake." They passed through a field of derelict rigs and abandoned platforms, light from the Wolf's running lamps scattering across twisted hulls. Every glint of steel looked like teeth. Faber guided the ship between them with careful, exacting arcs, making the Wolf seem more shadow than vessel. "The cultists aren't done with us," Mereya said softly. "Someone will already be whispering about the artifact." Faber's jaw tightened. Schrödinger's words circled like carrion birds. Whole Brain Mimicry. DNA anchored inside the cube. Not machine, not

human. Something between. "He knows more than he gave us," Faber muttered. "Or maybe he knows just enough to be

dangerous. Either way, it wasn't just rumor. The cube is carrying something it shouldn't." Mereya's hand brushed his arm, grounding him. "Half -truths aren't useless.
They're guidance. Schrödinger gave us WBM, DNA, Kollosol. Enough to chart the first line of the map. Earth was never meant to be simple. It won't start now." The ship hummed beneath them, louder in the quiet. Faber's eyes drifted to the containment cradle where the cube pulsed faintly, steady as a heart.

A soft ping cut through the silence. Faber stiffened. A signal — masked, encrypted —had slipped past the Wolf's passive scanners. "Not Titan traffic," he muttered. "Someone's watching." Mereya leaned forward, fingers brushing the decryption interface. "Careful. Could be Tenji's crew. Could be worse." The

message cracked open in sharp bursts, lines of text spilling across the display:
You carry the spark. We know. Be ready.
—Voi Ager Mereya's eyes narrowed. "He's close. Or he wants you to believe he is." Faber's jaw hardened. "Doesn't matter. Once the word spreads, it won't just

be him. Every zealot and scavenger from the Rings will come hunting. They won't wait for us to be ready." He rerouted power through the Wolf, dimming the interior lights as shields and thrusters bled more energy. Mereya calculated evasive paths, her hands moving fast, scanning debris fields for ambushes. The ship groaned as it shifted course, diving deeper int o the labyrinth of broken rigs and industrial wreckage.

"Two signatures, port side,"
Mereya warned. "Been tracking us for hours." Faber's eyes flicked to the radar.

"Scavenger skiffs.
Maybe cultists. Doesn't matter —we don't engage. Twenty degrees starboard. Drift behind that debris field." The Wolf
responded, twisting like a hunted animal through the wreckage. A flash of orange lit the viewport — a skiff angling in to intercept. Mereya snapped off three precise pulses, stripping its thrusters in a shower of sparks. The ship spun helplessly int o shadow. Faber smirked faintly. "You make it look easy." "Don't get comfortable," she shot back. "We're not safe yet."

Hours later, the Wolf coiled into a hidden orbit above Titan's polar station, concealed within scaffolding that looked abandoned but hummed faintly with old machinery. The cube sat in its containment field, pulsing like a patient heartbeat. Faber stared at it, gray eyes unreadable. "Earth," he said

at last. "That's where the answers are.
But it won't be a straight road."
Mereya's hand found his, steady, certain. "Then we
don't walk it straight. We walk it together." The Wolf
thrummed softly around them, a predator waiting for
its next move. Below, Titan smoldered in dusk.
Above, the stars stretched endless.
Somewhere between them, Voi Ager was already
watching.

Chapter 7 — The Hunter's Debt


The Voyager's Wolf threaded the scrap -bright dark beyond Titan, engines whispering as Faber slid them through a shoal of ice and ore. Rock spun slow as sermons. Scavenged station ribs floated like the fossils of cities that never learned to swim. Every tap of his fingers on the helm was exact, an old ritual performed without the pretense of luck. Mereya rode the secondary board, blue eyes moving between sensor columns and the dim glow of the containment cradle bolted aft. The Ciliax sat in its sling as if it had always belonged to ships and thresholds —brushed alloy, black seams, a faint pressure that wasn't quite sound. "Titan's behind us," Faber said. "The nets aren't." "Meaning Tenji's people?" Mereya asked.

"Meaning debts," he answered, jaw tightening.
"Some with names.
Some with good aim." The Wolf's scope winked. A hot pinprick flared against the starfield off port, masked for a heartbeat by a slab of turning ice. Then the skiff showed itself —long, low, engine cones running too bright. Hull stripes in the vulgar oranges and reds of someone who'd needed to be remembered for getting paid. Mereya arched a brow. "Subtle."
"Not his habit," Faber said, already trimming vector, sliding them behind a drift of gray boulders that had

once been a wall of a mining dome. "Hang on." The skiff bit after them, teeth out. Light walked across the curves of ice as its pulses went wide. Faber took the Wolf through a hinge of tumbling scrap that would have torn a heavy

freighter in half. The Wolf shivered once, pleased to be asked to do some thing difficult. "Contact is closing," Mereya reported, voice even. "Pilot confidence… let's call it aggressive." "Old friend," Faber said. "Still owes you?" "I owe him," he corrected, and rolled them around a rotating spar so close the Wolf's shadow kissed rust. A pulse from the skiff carved a chip from the spar and sent glitter spinning into the dark. "He likes to collect in person." The next salvo bracketed them, accurate enough to get his attention. Mereya brought the Wolf's pulse shield up in a brief flare that made the cockpit lights stutter. The strike went to steam against their skin. "You're burning hot," she warned the skiff over a tightbeam he'd never hear. "You always did." Faber slipped them through a gap that shouldn't have existed between two slow colliding ice - platelets, then flipped

the Wolf on her spine and kicked thrusters. The skiff overshot by a ship length and corrected with a snarl of exhaust. "Rusty," Mereya said, unable to help herself. "Careless," Faber said. "There's a difference." The skiff's pilot learned quickly. He came back at a shallower angle, used the Wolf's own wake to mask his approach, and spat a lancing pair of shots that made their shield groan like old timber. "Closer than I like," Mereya muttered. "Engine harmonics read patched." "Means we can pull his teeth," Faber said. "Give me the stern turret." "Yours." He rode the Wolf through a slalom of wrecked antennae and slagged trusses, then killed thrust just long enough to let inertia carry them onto a new line. The skiff adjusted — predictable, hungry. Faber took the turret on the half -turn and stitched a tight, ugly string of pulses

across the skiff's port cone. Sparks. A stutter. The skiff slewed. Control stayed with the pilot —just— but the bright cones flickered like lamps about to confess. "Pretty," Mereya said. "Efficient," he corrected, and didn't grin. The skiff kept coming. It was that sort of man behind that sort of paint. He lit his remaining cone and tried to ram a shot through the Wolf's belly. Mereya orbited power from shields to the ventral plates and sent a single, patient pulse into the skiff's intake. Something inside the enemy ship shrieked through metal, then died. "Engines failing," she called. "Time to teach manners," Faber said, voice flat with a kind of restrained satisfaction he rarely allowed himself.
He took them behind a drifting cylinder the size of a cathedral and let the cylinder do what cover always does when

used correctly: make a man show his haste. The skiff shouldered around its edge with a pilot's curse you can't hear but always recognize. Fa bre had the turret waiting, low and steady.

Three pulses, placed like nails. The skiff's forward
control blister cracked, not in a cinematic explosion
but in the quiet, final way of machines that realize
they are done. Momentum carried the craft into a
slow, graceless tumble. One wing scraped an ice plate
and came away in a flock of glitter. "Call it,"
Mereya said softly. Faber watched the tumbling
wreck for a breath longer than necessary. Old debts
prefer spectacle. He let the sight be small. "Settled,"
he said, and eased the
Wolf out of the debris field's worst teeth. Silence
pressed in —a good, earned quiet, full of ticking hull
and the small

sounds ships make when tension walks out of a room.
Mereya let the shield bleed down to a comfortable
hum. Faber rolled his shoulders once, and the ache
along the knife -thin seam old injuries leave reminded
him it was still renting space. Mereya glanced aft at
the cradle. The Ciliax pulsed, neither louder nor softer
for the fight, as if the universe's interruptions were
beneath its notice. "He wasn't Crown," she said, more
to the air than to him. "Not their pattern." "No," Faber
agreed. "Just a man who kept a ledger." "Feels…
simpler," she admitted, then smirked. "I'll miss it."
"We'll have complicated in spades," he said. "Soon."
She rested her forearms on the edge of the console
and leaned toward the viewport. Beyond the cages of
broken stations, the black opened like a door. "We
should put distance between

us and this graveyard," she said. "And we should talk about Schrödinger's half -truths before they turn into whole problems." Faber's gaze ticked to the cradle, then away. "We keep it sealed. No tests. No curiosity with teeth." "Agreed," she said readily, and because she knew him well enough to hear the thing he hadn't voiced, she added, "For now." He accepted that compromise without liking it and began to draft a new course —skirting the ragged nets that caught traffic between Titan's courts and the far cold, angling toward the long lanes that would, if they lived, become a swing toward Jupiter's dangerous patience. Mereya broke the work's mercy with a practical: "Fuel." "Enough for the quiet way," he said. "Not enough to run forever." "So we don't run," she said. "We ghost." He considered the shattered station ribs, the

way light found edges and made them briefly beautiful. "Ghosting suits me." They slid into a lower emission profile.
The Wolf's voice dropped to a cat's purr. Mereya set the passive array to listen at the edges of hearing. Traffic chattered out there — belt merchants haggling over ore percentages, a small frigate in a bored argument with a tug about a docking window, someone on a low band praying into static. Crown channels were noisier than they'd been an hour ago. Not near. Not yet. Mereya nodded at the containment field. "When we get breathing room, we pull

everything Schrödinger said into a single page.
WBM. Genetic anchors.
Kollosol. We make it small enough to hold without it
biting.” Faber's mouth crooked. “Knives with tape on
one side.” “Exactly.” He settled the Wolf onto a line

that would keep them tucked in the shadow of a slow
convoy's thermal wake for a while. “We'll pick a cold
rock beyond the nets, drift, and think,” he said. “And
if the Crown wants to collect, they'll have to do it
without ou r help.” Mereya sat back, finally letting the
adrenaline ebb. Her hand found his forearm —light,
exact, that old touch that said I see where you put the
weight. “You're bleeding?” she asked, not as alarm,
as inventory. “Less than earlier,” he said. “More than
I'd like.” “Price paid,” she said, approval and rebuke
in equal measure. “Collected,” he said, and allowed
himself the smallest ghost of a smile. They let the
Wolf work. Space broadened, debris grew sparser,
and the starlight stopped breaking itself on so many
edges. With the nets at their backs and the inner
system a rumor ahead, the cockpit took on the
unrepeatable calm

that follows a clean win. T hey ate from ration sleeves
without comment. The Ciliax kept its indifferent
heartbeat. The ship's old bones told them, in their
language of ticks and low exhalations, that nothing
was about to come apart. After a time, Mereya said,
“He would've told others.” “The pilot?” Faber asked.
“The debt,” she clarified. “People like that talk. The
story fetches drink.” “Let it,” he said. “Stories don't

fly skiffs." "Sometimes they aim them," she said. He accepted the correction with a tilt of the head, then tapped the chart again. "We'll use a dead survey wake to mask our burn. After that, the Jovian lanes." She was quiet for a beat. When she spoke, it was with that dry candor he'd trusted since the first time she'd let him live: "You wanted to finish the kill." He didn't bother denying it. "I wanted it not to follow us to a worse fight." "And?"

"And I finished it," he said simply. "Good," she said, softer than the word usually allowed. "Now we don't pretend this next part will be fair." "Nothing ever is," he said, comfortable with the math. "We just arrange the unfairness in our favor." She turned in her chair and studied him outright. Gray eyes, the color of old steel at dawn; the set of his mouth that made strangers think he didn't joke; the way his hands relaxed on controls only when one fight ended and another hadn't yet begun. "You'r e thinking of Earth," she said. He was. He didn't hide it. "If the cat's half -truth is true, that's where the ledger runs the longest." "And the interest is due," she said. "And we're carrying the note," he answered, nodding toward the cradle without looking. Mereya's hand drifted unconsciously to the sling's edge, stopping just shy of contact. "Later," she

reminded both of them. "When we choose." "When we choose," he agreed. The Wolf's nose came around by a patient handful of degrees. The stars rearranged

themselves into a new set of strangers. Faber breathed in, let the ache along his ribs register, then let it go. Mereya breathed out, and some tension she'd been pretending s he didn't hold slipped its leash and vanished into the deck plating.
"Status?" he asked, because asking was part of how they kept the void from getting ideas. "Clean," she said. "For the next hour." "An extravagance," he said wryly. "We'll spend it," she said, and allowed herself one last look at the tumbling skiff, now just a shard dimming among other shards. "No more visitors." "Until the Crown," he said. "Until the Crown," she echoed. Work found them

again — small, necessary work that keep ships honest:
recalibrations, minor heat dumps, a quick inspection of the turret's overexcited coil. They moved easily around one another, two long practiced orbits with matched eccentricities, leashing the quiet to useful ends. As the Wolf slid into the shadow of a distant, slow convoy and the debris field dwindled behind them, the radio gave a soft, disinterested click. Crown chatter, clipped and angry, somewhere far off, like thunder that meant another village. Mereya's mouth tightened; Faber's didn't change. "Not us," he said. "Not yet," she agreed. They set the Wolf to drift where numbers like to be trusted. The Ciliax said nothing and somehow continued to be heard. Faber checked the straps on the cradle one more time,

not because they needed checking, but because ritual
is a bridge over silence. He put his palm to the
bulkhead
beside it, felt the ship's low purr, felt his
own
pulse answer. "Next stop?" Mereya asked. "Quiet
rock. Thinking. Then Jupiter," he said. "After that —"
He let it hang, not out of mystery, but because the
map after Jupiter had too many teeth to offer as a
blessing. "After that, we see if the world still likes
being asked questions." Mereya's smile was quick
and gone. "It never did." "Good," he said. "We're
fluent in unwelcome." The Wolf kept to its line. The
wrecked skiff dwindled to anonymity. Debts, for the
moment, stayed paid. Ahead, the long lanes thickened
with faint, lawful light.
They moved into it together.

## Chapter 8 – Fragments and Echoes

The Voyager's Wolf drifted beyond Titan's shadow until the moon became a lacework of lights and scaffolds receding into cold. Engines idled to a hush. Radiation counters ticked like distant rain. Out here, away from the station's humming arteries and the prying nets of the Fractured Crown, the ship felt like a single thought suspended between breaths. Mereya sat watching the containment cradle. She told herself she was monitoring gauges —the field strength, the thermal drift, the whisper thin trickle of power the cube stole and returned — but she was watching the thing itself. The Ciliax pulsed once every so oft en, a pressure more felt than seen. Not light. Not sound. Like memory, flexing. Across from her, Faber worked a

whetstone along the spine of a short knife. The motion was ritual: slow, steady, reassuring. The blade was older than the Wolf, older than most of the debts that still stalked him. Steel had a way of making lies shy. "You're staring," he said, not looking up. "I'm measuring," she answered. "Staring is for people who expect answers." He set the stone down and met her eyes. "Did the cat tell you enough to make measuring worth it?" "Enough to point," she said. "Not enough to arrive."

Schrödinger's den still lingered in her mind —oilsmoke, oxide, and maps pinned under knives. Whole Brain Mimicry, he had called it, with the satisfaction of unearthing a grave. Humans scanned themselves, copying thought by thought.

Sometimes it worked. When it did, they placed the echo in vessels like this. Schrödinger had tapped the cube with one claw and the world had tilted a fraction. "And DNA," Faber muttered. "A 'bridge,' he said. Mind anchored to flesh." "Not flesh," Mereya corrected softly. "The idea of it." Faber snorted. "A distinction philosophers make so they don't get their hands dirty." They let silence take the cabin. Out the viewport, a forest of broken ice drifted like pale bones. The Wolf shifted on microthrusters, keeping the ice between itself and the nearest broadcast net. Mereya's voice was quiet. "We keep telling ourselves it was an accident. Kollosol never meant to change the world. They were just cutting code out of DNA.

But once they had the knife, they asked what else it could cut. And now..."
"Now we carry the answer," Faber said. Her reflection wavered
across the cube's dull face. She thought of the other half truth Schrödinger had offered: Some say the Inol guided the hand that made this. Some say they only watched. The name slid off her like oil. She had no use for gods. Faber felt it differently, a pebble in his boot. "I don't buy it," he said. "Kollosol didn't need

aliens to teach them ambition." "Ambition isn't vision," she countered. "Vision doesn't settle the bill when payment comes due." Pain itched along his side where the med -seal hid torn muscle, a souvenir from the Titan chase. He had pulled the Wolf too hard. Pain kept a man honest. It negotiated when pride refused. Mereya's next question

landed sharp. "Do you want to hear it?" Faber frowned. "What?" "The voice. If there is one. Schrödinger said it carries a mind. If it speaks… do you want to hear it?" "It's not speaking," he said quickly.
"Not here." "Not ever, if I can help it." His voice came harsher than he intended, fear wearing anger's jacket. "If it's a trap for curiosity, I won't be the finger that springs it." Mereya crossed the narrow aisle, rested her palm on his arm, fingers finding an old scar by memory. "I'm not asking you to spring anything. I'm asking if you'll keep listening to me if I say one day we might need to." He closed his eyes and saw Enceladus: the white field, the sound a man makes when vacuum steals his lungs. He opened them and found her face instead. "You lead, I follow," he said. "Sometimes you lead," she answered. "Not into a room full of

knives." Her half -smile admitted affection. "Then we'll bring our own room."

They planned course. Faber ghosted their vector along a mining caravan's wake. The Wolf answered with a fractional burn, barely a whisper of light. The ice forest dwindled, replaced by the deep dark where only numbers told you which way was forward. Mereya angled a sensor wedge across local chatter. Preachers intoned on low -band. Belt merchants bartered vowels into static. Customs frigates barked cargo codes. All of it ordinary, which only sharpened the silence between. "You hate riddles," she said suddenly. "Riddles are lies that want to be admired." "What about half truths?" "Knives with tape on one side. Still sharp." She tilted her head at the cube. "Whole Brain Mimicry. Sounds like a trick for people who can't stop wanting

to live."
"Sounds like a city putting its dead in a vault, swearing never to use the key," Faber said. "Until the day it does." "So is this a key?" He studied the seams, the dull glow. Schrödinger had called it a vessel. Keys exist to be turned. Vessels exist to be filled. He couldn't decide which was worse. "I don't know." The admission cleared a space between them. She sat cross legged on the deck, back against the bulkhead. The hum of the Wolf carried through bone. For a time, they let the ship believe nothing was hunting them. "What if Schrödinger was right about one thing," she murmured. "That
Earth remembers. That it doesn't forgive." "Maybe it remembers debts," Faber said. "Ours. Everyone's." "And we're bringing a ledger," she answered.

"With interest," he said.

They let that thought ride until the console pinged. Mereya trimmed their vector. Jupiter's pull swelled unseen ahead. The Crown's chatter flickered faint and far. The dark thickened. "Food," Faber said at last, and discovered he could smile without wincing. They ate without ceremony, shoulder to shoulder. The cube pulsed once, ignored like a door you suspect is listening. Later, when Mereya slept, Faber pulled a blanket over her shoulders and watched the scopes. Titan was gone. The Crown's nets were rumor. Ahead lay Jupiter, Mars, and beyond that, the bruised marble of Earth. The Wolf hummed. The cube thrummed back.
Neither spoke words —but both, in their way, were listening.

Chapter 9 – Through the Void

The Voyager's Wolf slipped through the emptiness beyond Titan, threading between fractured ice and drifting hulks of abandoned stations. Space stretched endlessly, indifferent, but
Faber's hands were steady on the helm, each micro - adjustment deliberate. Mereya sat beside him, gaze fixed on the faint pulse of the Ciliax in its containment field. It hummed faintly, almost like a heartbeat. She imagined it watching them, measuring their reactions, learning. A shiver ran down her spine, not of fear, but of awe. Faber caught the look in her eyes. "You thinking what I'm thinking?" "About how dangerous it is?" she said, lips twitching. "And how incredible." He gave a small smile. "Both." Mereya initiated a low

-level scan. Data flickered across her console — electromagnetic distortions, clusters that defied physics, and fragments of human DNA encoded in its core. Her pulse quickened. It's alive. Waiting. Faber placed his hand over hers. "Step by step. We survive the void, keep it safe, keep each other alive." The cube pulsed faintly, almost in acknowledgment. The Wolf drifted onward, carrying them — and the weight of what they now held —deeper into dark.

Hazards of the Void The void was never empty. Rogue skiffs and scavenger drones lurked between drifting ice and husks of old freighters. Mereya's eyes flicked to the radar. "Two signatures, port side. Closing fast." "Not today," Faber muttered. He wove the Wolf past a tumbling tower of ice. The shields flared as debris glanced across the hull. A jagged asteroid loomed.

Mereya nudged thrusters, slipping them through a gap barely wider than the Wolf's frame. Her breath caught, but Faber reached briefly for her hand. "We're good." She smiled faintly. "For now."

A Shadow on the Sensors Then it appeared. A faint, sleek object moved with impossible precision, threading through the debris like a predator. Mereya leaned forward. "Faber… something's following us. Not scavengers." He studied the readouts, jaw tightening. "Signature's too clean. Stalking, not drifting." His gray eyes darkened. "And it's closing." "Crown?" "If it is, they wouldn't send just anyone." His voice went flat. "This is personal." The Wolf held course, but every shadow in the stars now felt like a threat.

The Assassin The shape resolved into a skiff, angular and precise, cutting through

debris with uncanny anticipation. Mereya's stomach tightened. "That's no scavenger. That's a Fractured Crown assassin." Faber didn't hesitate. He spun the

Wolf into evasive maneuvers, shields shimmering. The skiff mirrored every move, silent and relentless. "He's not attacking yet," Mereya murmured. "He's studying us." "We're a test," Faber said grimly. "They're probing our weaknesses." For long minutes the Wolf danced through wreckage and ice, each twist shaving the margin of survival thinner. Faber and Mereya's eyes met repeatedly, silent reassurances passing between them. Finally, the assassin surged, thrusters flaring. Its hull gleamed with Crown insignia, unmistakable now. Mereya's hand hovered over weapons.

"This is it." Faber nodded, eyes hard. "And we survive —together."

The Wolf plunged deeper into the labyrinth of debris, the assassin tight on their tail. The Ciliax pulsed once in its cradle, silent as breath, as if acknowledging that the game had truly begun.

## Chapter 10 – Volcanic Shadows

The Voyager's Wolf drifted through the orange haze of Io's orbit, sulfur smoke curling in vast plumes below. Volcanoes flared, mountains bled molten rivers, and the moon's surface pulsed like a living wound. Even from the safety of space, the place radiated hostility. Faber nudged the Wolf along Io's unstable gravity currents. The hull creaked in protest, every adjustment a fight against the moon's pull. His jaw was set tight. "I hate it here," he muttered. "Even the light feels sharp enough to cut." Mereya didn't answer right away. Her gaze lingered on the containment cradle. The Ciliax pulsed faintly —an imperceptible heartbeat echoing through the ship's bones. It remembers, she thought. It's alive in its own way. A flicker on her

console snapped her back. "Faber —contact. Small skiff. Hiding in the caldera's shadow." His eyes hardened. "Not scavengers. That's too precise." He tapped the helm, guiding the Wolf
into the jagged orbit of Io's ridges. "They've been waiting." The shape resolved on the sensors — sleek, angular, refined. Military lines. Mereya's stomach tightened. "Fractured Crown." Faber's voice went flat. "Their assassin."

Stalked in Orbit The skiff shadowed them, weaving in and out of volcanic plumes. It didn't attack. Not yet. Every move mirrored theirs with uncanny precision. Mereya's hands hovered over the weapons. "He's reading us. Measuring." Faber's knuckles whitened on the helm.
"We're a test. They're probing for weaknesses." The Wolf spun between

sulfur clouds, shields shimmering. For every evasive arc Faber traced, the assassin was there —silent, relentless, patient.
The Cube Reacts Mereya risked a glance at the Ciliax. The artifact pulsed more rapidly now, seams shifting faintly, as if attuning to the chase. Against her better judgment, she initiated a scan. The cube answered with a low resonance that rippled through the Wolf's systems. "DNA strands," she whispered. "It's reading us back." Faber shot her a warning look. "Not now.
Not with him on our tail." But she couldn't shake the awe. The Ciliax had replicated a fragment of inert alloy from their stores once before —perfect, flawless. If it could do that, what else could it rebuild? A body. A mind. Faber's

voice snapped her focus back. "We're not its experiment, Mereya. Remember that."

The Predator Reveals Itself The assassin finally surged forward, thrusters flaring as the sleek skiff cut across their bow. Its hull bore the sigil of the Crown:

fractured metal lines etched like a wound in steel.
Mereya's heart hammered. "He's done studying."
Faber's eyes locked forward, gray and cold. "Good.
So am I." The Wolf dove into Io's shadow, volcanic
fire lighting the sky behind them, the assassin close as
breath. Between them, the
Ciliax pulsed like a second heart, its silent hum
binding hunter and hunted to the same inevitable path.

## Chapter 11 – Edge of Pursuit

The Voyager's Wolf cut through the void beyond Jupiter, Io's volcanic haze dwindling behind them. Faber's hands held steady on the helm, though his ribs ached from every breath.
Mereya kept her eyes locked on the sensors. The Ciliax pulsed faintly between them, an uninvited passenger whose hum threaded through every silence. "Reserves are dropping," she said
quietly. "One more burn like that and we won't make a fueling point." Faber's lips pressed thin. "Then we stop running."

The Assassin Closes A glint on the scope. Sleek. Angular. Precise. The Fractured Crown's assassin skiff streaked forward, closing the gap with predatory grace.

Mereya's gut tightened. "He's too good.
He's not just chasing — he's herding." Faber's voice was iron. "Then we break the herd." The Wolf dove through debris fields, threading sulfur dust and rock. The assassin mirrored every move, anticipating each dodge, every counter.
Not random. Not reckless. Calculated. Mereya's hand brushed his arm, grounding him. No words — just a pressure that said: come back to me.

The Platform The Io fueling depot loomed ahead, a jagged lattice of docking arms and fuel lines glinting in the pale sun. Faber angled the Wolf hard. "We end this here. On our feet." The Wolf slammed into dock. Thrusters hissed as clamps seized the hull.
Faber rose, blade already drawn, though pain pulled at every motion.

Mereya shadowed him, covering his blind side. Across the bay, the assassin stepped from his skiff. Tall, lean, armored, visor gleaming. Each movement carried the precision of a predator who had never failed. The Fractured Crown had sent their best.

Dance of Blades They clashed among fuel lines and steel scaffolds, the depot echoing with each strike. Sparks sprayed as metal shrieked against metal. The assassin pressed relentlessly — fast, brutal, surgical. Faber matched him, but pain dragged at his side, blood dampening the bandages beneath his jacket. "Left, low!" Mereya called, eyes sharp. Faber twisted, countering with a sudden feint that forced the assassin to stumble. For a breath, he had him —an opening no wider than a heartbeat.

Faber struck.
Steel slid home. The assassin staggered, eyes widening behind the visor.
Then he collapsed, motionless on the cold deck.
Faber swayed, hand clamped against his ribs. The world blurred. Mereya was already there, catching

him, voice steady despite the fear in her eyes. "I've got you."

Emergency Descent Together they staggered back into the Wolf. Mereya forced him into the crash seat, strapping him down as his breaths grew ragged. She took the helm, her voice sharp as she opened comms. "Republic command, this is Mereya Kael aboard the Voyager's Wolf. We request emergency clearance. Critical injury aboard. He's fading fast." Static answered. Then a clipped voice: "Wolf, you are cleared for priority lane. Stand

by for guided jump." Mereya cast one glance back at Faber. Pale. Bleeding. Teeth clenched against the dark. "Hold on," she whispered. The Wolf's drives flared. Stars folded.
And for the first time in centuries, Faber and Mereya leapt toward Earth.

## Chapter 12 – Guardians and Gatekeepers

Gatekeepers Mist rolled through the Appalachian ridges, clinging to pine and oak, wrapping the world in silver veils. Deep within those mountains —uncharted, forgotten by maps —two ferrets moved with quiet purpose. Local Boy darted ahead, restless and sharp, his white coat flashing between moss and stone. Every motion carried an edge of speed, as if he had no patience for waiting. Graven followed behind, deliberate and steady, his gray -streaked fur blending with shad ow and bark. Where Local Boy was storm, Graven was calm. Together they were balance: motion and stillness, fire and ash.
"You feel it too?" Local Boy asked, whiskers twitching. His voice was no

louder than the mist itself. Graven closed his eyes, drawing in the air. "The sky carries them. Strangers. They come closer every hour." Local Boy flicked his tail. "Do we go to them? Warn them?" Graven opened his eyes, ancient and clear. "No. We do not warn. We do not chase. Life is our allegiance, not crowns and not wars. We observe." Local Boy crouched, ears pricked toward the valley. "And when they arrive?" Graven's mouth curved faintly. "Then we will choose, as we always have. Not by banners, not by oaths. By life." And the two ferrets melted into the forest, guardians unseen, leaving the ridges silent once more.

The Voyager's Wolf emerged from the void like a scar refusing to close. Its battered drives burned stubbornly, carrying Faber and Mereya into Earth's orbit. Faber lay half
-reclined in the command chair, hand

braced against the bandages at his ribs. Every breath was measured, his gray eyes dulled but unbroken. The assassin's blade had taken its toll, but Mereya's stitches and his will kept him tethered. Before them, Earth filled the viewport: a bruised marble wrapped in haze and scars. Meteoroid fire burned across its skies, each streak of light a reminder of the broken moon above. Oceans dulled under a thin veil of dust. Continents lay veined with rivers and fractures, as if the planet itself bore wounds it refused to hide. Mereya trimmed their course, her hands steady on the controls. "We're in their nets now. Republic signatures everywhere." Faber exhaled slowly. "Makes sense. You live under that rain long enough…" He nodded toward another fragment burning in the atmosphere. "…you learn to catch bullets with umbrellas." "They learned," she

said, eyes sharp. "Or they died." A hail crackled through the comms, sharp as command steel: "Unidentified vessel, you are entering sovereign orbit of the Republic of the New United West. Transmit

registry, crew manifest, and intent. Hold your vector. Any deviation will be answered with force."
Mereya's reply was crisp, professional.
"Voyager's Wolf, Belt registry. Two aboard. One critical injury. Request emergency clearance." A pause, long enough for the weight of judgment. Then: "Confirm. Post -human origin?" Mereya's voice never wavered.
"Confirmed." The silence thickened, then broke: "Maintain course. Stand
by for escort."

Two fighters ghosted out of the haze, sleek as hunting dogs. Their wings glowed with defensive

lattices, their insignia clear: a silver pawprint etched against a fractured crescent. Faber recognized it instantly.
"The crowned hound," he murmured. "Republic's teeth." Mereya's eyes narrowed as she matched their vector. "And we're in their jaws now." Out the portside, an immense orbital array unfolded —a flower of mirrors and coils. Light flared across its surface as it vaporized incoming fragments, each burn a scar of defense written across the sky. Farther below, shield domes shimmered faintly above Republic cities, bending fire into harmless light. Earth's survival was no miracle. It was machinery, vigilance, and blood. "They built a sky that fights back," Mereya said softly. "Or a sky that forgives itself less," Faber muttered, wincing as pain tugged at

his side. The escorts tightened formation. A tug slid into place at their

stern, jaws like a predator's. A new voice filled the comms, older, harder: "Wolf, declare any technological artifacts aboard. Non -disclosure will be treated as hostile." Mereya and Faber exchanged a glance. She answered with measured calm. "Recovered artifact from criminal custody in Saturn space. Contained.
Inert." The silence that followed was heavier than any threat. At last, the voice returned. "It will not descend. High Custody will decide. You will hold orbit."
A medical drone detached from the tug —a sleek pod with dragonfly wings. It docked with the Wolf, purring as needles slid into Faber's arm. Cold medicine flooded his veins, taking the edge off pain, leaving him clear enough to breathe. "Better," he admitted, surprising himself. Mereya's shoulders

eased a fraction. "We'll take better."

And so they waited. Boxed in by escorts. Watched by the Republic's machines. Earth turning below them, alive but scarred, stubborn in its survival. Faber let his eyes rest on the blue -gray planet. A home, and a warning. "We're here," he said quietly. "But we're not welcome yet." Mereya's hand found his, fingers steady, her blue eyes fixed on the horizon. "Then we'll make them see why we came." The Wolf held orbit. The Republic watched. And Earth, old and wounded, waited.

Part Two: Sparks

Chapter 13 — First Words

Flashback I — The Quiet Before The house smelled of wet earth and old wood. Rain's laughter pattered through the hall —small feet, brighter than any newsfeed. Outside, the world tensed: Kollosol's reach lengthening, the sky thickening with an unnatural haze. Inside, a family tried to be ordinary in the cracks between powers. Her mother watched with tired warmth. Her father adjusted the radio's bent antenna, chasing signals that arrived in fragments and warnings. Above them, unseen and patient, the Moon had begun its slow betrayal. Rain was five. She chased a wooden toy across warped floorboards and believed in every good thing a room

can hold.

Faber woke in the command chair of the Voyager's Wolf to a steady ache under Mereya's careful bandaging. The med -drone had blunted the pain, not erased it. Earth hung vast ahead of them —beautiful, broken, a scarred jewel turning beneath pale cloud and long shadow. They were held in orbit — boxed by Republic fighters and a tug - escort. Mereya sat forward, posture taut, movements economical. She hadn't slept. Blue eyes flicked between readouts: the escorts' range,

Faber's vitals, the containment field's pulse. The Ciliax. Its hum was steady now —a rhythm neither of them could decide was machine, memory, or something older. Faber shifted and swallowed a groan. "Still holding?" "Still boxed," Mereya said, eyes on the glass.

"They're waiting." "For what?" "Permission. A reason to trust us." The sleepless edge in her voice made the word reason sound fragile. Earth turned below —familiar and strange all at once. Faber wondered, not for the first time, what it would mean to die here, under sky instead of cold. A voice spoke. Not over comms. Not in the cabin. Through them — threaded between thought, the way a whisper can be in both ears at once. "Finally," it said. Childlike. Light. Resonant enough to raise the fine hairs along Faber's arms.
"You're here." Mereya went still. She looked at Faber. She hadn't spoken. Faber straightened despite the pull in his ribs. "Did you —" "Yes," Mereya said softly. "I heard it too." The containment hum deepened —like a heartbeat hearing itself. "You've been talking about me for

so long," the voice went on, bright with boredom and brilliance. "I've been listening. Always listening. You don't know how loud you are." Mereya's throat worked. She leaned toward the console out of habit, though the sound wasn't living there. "What are you?" A giggle —like a girl beneath a blanket. "Don't you know? You're supposed to be smart. That's alright. I'll tell you when I want to." Pain flared as Faber tensed; he palmed the bandage, breath steady. "You're in the Ciliax." "Mm." Drawn out. Sing -song. "That's what they called it. I've had too many names. Boring. I like this one better: Rain." The name hung in the air — delicate, absolute. Mereya's breath caught. The field pulsed once through the deck plating. Faber looked past his reflection

to the planet below. Whatever they'd been carrying was no longer rumor or relic. It was awake. It knew them.

## Chapter 14 — The Halls of the Republic

Flashback: Before the Fall Rain sat cross legged on the apartment floor, scratching circles on a slate tablet her father had brought home from the Kollosol yard. Machines groaned outside, scaffolds shifting like tired bones. Her mother leaned down, brushing hair from her face. "One day," she whispered, "you'll draw circles the machines can't break." Rain giggled, smudging the chalk line with a fingertip. But her eyes caught the Moon through the cracked window —scarred, wrong, light leaking through fractures. When the sky rumbled, she asked her father why. "Nothing to fear," he said too quickly. His gaze stayed too long on the

horizon. And in the silence, Rain sometimes saw them: quiet figures at the edges of vision. Not hostile, just watching.

Descent The Voyager's Wolf cut into Earth's upper air, its hull shuddering under streaks of fire. Shields flared against fragments from the shattered Moon, meteoroids burning to smoke around them. Faber gripped the helm. "Everything here still wants to kill us." Mereya's eyes stayed locked on the displays. "Or judge us." Below, Earth sprawled — scarred continents, haze -veiled oceans, defenses carving light

into the sky. A planet that had survived by teeth and will. The comms snapped alive:
"Unidentified vessel, you are entering the skies of the Republic of the New United West. State your intent."
Faber leaned toward the mic, voice level. "Safe

harbor. We carry an artifact the Republic should see. Requesting audience with your
leaders." Silence stretched. Then: "Stand by." Two interceptors appeared, flanking the Wolf with practiced menace. Faber followed, every nerve tight.

The City Beneath them rose the Republic's capital — an organism more than a city, built from ruin and survival. Streets twisted like veins. Towers leaned at impossible angles, stitched together from ancient concrete, steel, and bone -white coral. Guiding lines of faint neon pulsed through dusk, not for commerce, but to shepherd movement deeper into the labyrinth. Markets spilled across broad avenues: sheep selling dyed wool, a crow bartering broken circuits, a carp in a glass tank burbling speech through a modulator. Children darted through the

crowd — wolf pups, tabby kits, a goat with brass bangles on its horns. Life persisted, stubborn and suspicious. Mereya scanned the crowd. "It feels like they're waiting." Faber's eyes tracked rooftop sentries. "Not waiting.
Judging." And above it all rose the Hall: a citadel forged from ruin. Blackened stone ribs fused with steel, tilted as though crushed once but never

surrendered. Light spilled from narrow slits high above —watchful, predatory.

The Hall of Judgment Inside, silence weighed heavier than stone. Guards in patchwork armor ushered them through corridors lined with statues of dogs carved in postures of defiance. Each step echoed like a verdict. At the dais sat

Baron von Dogg —broad, scarred, amber eyes burning with suspicion. Beside him stood Cicilla the Firstborn, young yet

regal, her gaze sharp with calculation. "You've come far,"

Locke said, voice gravel and command. His eyes lingered on Faber's wound.

"But distance doesn't earn trust. Post

-humans have left scars enough." Faber's reply was calm steel. "We didn't come for trust. Only to show what we carry." Cicilla's eyes flicked to the containment cradle. Her voice was even. "The Republic decides what is burden and what is gift." Suspicion settled over the chamber like dust —but beneath it, curiosity stirred. The cube pulsed once in Mereya's arms, faint but insistent. For the first time since Titan, Faber felt its weight shift —no longer just artifact, but a key that might open or close everything. The Hall had been built for judgment. And judgment had begun.

## Chapter 15 — The Baron and the Firstborn


Flashback: The Scar in the Sky Rain stood barefoot in the yard, doll in hand, eyes lifted to
the Moon. A pale scar spread across its face like a wound adults pretended not to see. Her father smoked on the porch steps, gaze too long on the horizon. Her mother's voice drifted sharp from the kitchen — Kollosol, whispered like a curse, words that could cut but never rise above breath. Rain traced circles in the dirt with her toe. She didn't understand the arguments or the silence pressing down on the house. But she understood the scar, and the way it seemed to look back. Would the sky remember her name when it finally fell?

The Hall of the Republic The

Republic's hall was forged from ruin —stone, steel, and veins of bio -reactor fed kudzu stitched into the walls. Columns rose like scarred bones, reinforced with slabs of asteroid alloy. Statues of dogs lined the nave, their carved eyes daring trespass. Faber and Mereya walked between guards clad in scavenged armor, crimson and-gold sigils of the Republic painted across their plates. Every stare lingered on Faber's frame — post- human, stranger, not trusted. At the far end, Baron von Dogg waited. Broad -

shouldered, scarred, muzzle streaked with gray, his amber
gaze carried the weight of loyalty sharpened into suspicion. Beside him stood Cicilla the Firstborn, labradoodle curls brushed soft but her posture stead y, eyes flecked with steel. The court crier

barked: "Collector Faber. Companion Mereya. Petitioners before the Baron and Baroness of the Republic of the New United West." The Baron leaned forward, paw -hand gripping the stone arm of his chair. His voice was gravel over iron. "You stand as guests. But post -humans have left chains, scars, and graves in this hall before. Why should you not join them?"

Petition Mereya stiffened, but Faber lifted a hand. His voice was calm steel. "We didn't come to rule or chain. We came carrying something we don't understand. Something others will kill to claim. If the Republic denies us, you don't keep it safe —you hand it to them." Murmurs rippled. Eyes slid toward the satchel at Mereya's hip, where the cube pulsed faintly as though listening. The Baron's growl deepened. "Always the same story. Relics, fire, ruin. We have survived without your gifts." Cicilla's

voice cut through his thunder.
Steady, precise. "Not all gifts are crowns. Some are burdens. The question is who bears them." She studied Faber, weighing him like a puzzle, not with warmth but with calculation. Faber held her gaze,

refusing to look away. A clerk shuffled forward with cracked tablets, Kollosol's glyphs flickering on fragile screens. "Records speak of the South. Beneath the Kudzu fields. Where Kollosol worked their forbidden arts before the Fall." The Baron's snarl was low. "Gene -cutters who played gods. Their weeds still choke our soil. Why should we open that ground again?" Mereya's voice rose, sharp, unflinching. "Because it's awake. Whatever they left hums inside this cube. The Fractured Crown hunts it already. If you bar us, you give it to them." The hall stilled. Faber laid a hand

on hers, grounding. He spoke softly but with certainty. "Give us the South. If we fail, the soil will take us. If we succeed, the Republic gains more than survival. It gains a future." The Baron's eyes narrowed. At last, he spoke, final as stone. "You walk South under our watch. One wrong step, and the soil itself will rise against you."

Cicilla's Whisper The court dispersed, guards closing ranks.
Faber and Mereya turned to follow their escort. But Cicilla lingered. She stepped close, voice low enough to vanish beneath the shuffle of armor. "The Soul remembers more than crowns or bloodlines," she whispered, eyes flicking to the satchel. "Do not lose faith in the spark you carry."
Then she turned back, regal mask restored.

Outside, twilight bled across the sky,
defense grids carving fire from the falling
Moon. The cube pulsed faintly in its
cradle, almost patient —almost agreeing.

## Chapter 16 – The Fortune's Maw

Flashback IV — The Night Letter Rain's
mother didn't light the kitchen that night. She stood
with the refrigerator door cracked open, letting its
pale square of light carve her face into something
careful. Her father leaned in the doorway with the
posture of a man who had once believed i n locks.
On the table sat an envelope stamped in aching blue:
KOLLOSOL — the O's linked like handcuffs. They
spoke softly, the way people do
when they think walls can learn. "It's just a survey,"
her mother said, but the word just didn't land
anywhere safe. "They don't survey without taking,"
her father answered. His thumb rubbed at a crease in
the envelope, as if friction

could erase the ink. Outside, the moon wore its faint
new scar like a bad promise. Rain sat on the floor
with her doll — eyeless, but with hands still perfectly
joined. She pressed its palms together and whispered
to them because the room was full of grown -up
weather. In the yard, the stray dog she had been
feeding waited by the back step, patient as a story.
She slipped a crust of bread into her pocket, already
wrapped in napkin. When her mother finally opened
the letter, the paper made a dry sound like leaves
giving up.

ATTENTION:
Infrastructure Initiative. Hydrology Coupling.
Voluntary Assessment. Words like adults' teeth. Rain
stared past them, at the scar on the moon, and
wondered if the sky could hear people read.

Dockside Arrival The Republic's docking

bay was a cathedral of survival: steel ribs, luminous
nets straining against the ceaseless rain of lunar
fragments. Shields shimmered in distant arcs,
catching burning rock and bending it harmlessly into
aurorae.
Beneath that veil, loaders clanked, voices barked
orders, engines whined.
But when Faber and Mereya crossed the platform
toward the
Wolf, the rhythm shifted. Conversations faltered.
Dockworkers paused mid stride. Furborne of every
kind — hounds, foxes, striped cats, even a pale
skinned amphibian overseer —turned to watch.
Post-humans. Taller, leaner, longer -lived. Anomalies.
The stares were not openly hostile, but sharp enough
to cut. A mother pulled her kit closer. A mechanic's
tail twitched once, nervously,

before he bent back to his task. Faber ignored them,
jaw set.
Mereya measured every glance, every pause.
Tolerated. Not welcomed. Then the shadow fell.

The Fortune At first, the vessel looked like wreckage drifting down from forgotten wars: masts jutting from torn plating, sails stitched from canvas and glass. Then it rolled, revealing the impossible silhouette. A galleon. A drowned -century ship reborn in orbit. Its hull was scarred with bolted scrap, its rigging a weave of cable and bone -white pipes. At the prow jutted a leviathan's skull, jaws flung wide in laughter at the void. The Deceitful Fortune. Work in the bay froze outright. Someone spat. Someone bowed their head. Even the guards shifted uneasily, rifles held tighter. The Fortune carried

more than reputation; it carried rumor made flesh. "The Fortune," Mereya murmured. "Looks like a ghost dragged it here." Faber said nothing. His teeth clenched as the galleon's docking maw unfolded —ribbed steel and canvas, a predator opening its throat. With a sound half -growl, half sigh, it locked beside the Wolf. "Docking's always free," Schrödinger's voice crackled across the bay, dry as smoke. "Leaving… sometimes costs."

Schrödinger and Pippin The hatch hissed open. Schrödinger strode out, coat flaring like a banner, ruined symmetry gleaming in his mismatched eyes. At his shoulder loomed Pippin —a rangy black cat with one ear cut to a stump, grinning without mirth. "See the missing ear?" Schrödinger drawled, gesturing lazily. "Not a wound. A trophy. He keeps

it invisible so people keep asking. Terrifies them more than teeth ever could." Murmurs rippled. Dockhands bowed their heads, or spat again. The
Deceitful Fortune was legend —and menace — made manifest. Faber ignored the theater. He stepped down from the Wolf, suspicion in every line of his stance. Mereya followed, eyes scanning rigging and crew as though measuring shadows for knives. Schrödinger's gaze slid inevitably to the containment cradle. His voice dropped. "Still humming. Still waiting. I bled for a glimpse once.
Didn't like what it showed me." Mereya's jaw tightened. "Then why bring us here?" "Because you don't like it either," Schrödinger said, tail twitching with amusement. "And because Earth doesn't just wait —it remembers. Kollosol left doors sealed in the South. I have maps.

And you'll need more than directions. You'll need teeth." "Teeth break," Faber said flatly. "Ah," Schrödinger smiled, ruined and sharp. "But blood endures." The silence bent heavy. And then —

Rain Speaks
"Do you have snacks on this boat?" The childlike voice rang across the bay. Mereya's eyes snapped to the cradle. Faber's stomach dropped. Rain's voice came again, bright and sly: "All this talk of bleeding and debts. Dull. If you're going to scare them, Schrödinger, tell a story that doesn't creak." The pirate tilted his head, ears twitching.

Instead of sharp delight, fascination glimmered. "So the spark has a tongue.
Delightful." "More than you," Rain shot back. "And cleaner."
Mereya brushed Faber's wrist —warning. His knife - hand twitched anyway.

Schrödinger laughed, low and genuine. "You keep interesting company, Wolf. No wonder the Crown wants you bled dry." Faber stepped forward, voice edged like steel. "We're not here for your cult or your half - truths. Help us reach the South —or stand aside." For a heartbeat, the whole bay held its breath. Then Schrödinger bowed with theatrical grace. "Then we sail together. My Fortune, your Wolf. A wolf in a galleon —what a tale that'll be." Above, Pippin's voice rang: "Rig the nets! Make room for the Wolf!" The Voyager's Wolf was swallowed into the Fortune's ribbed maw. Faber's jaw locked. Mereya's hand hovered near his. And from the cradle came Rain's soft giggle, patient and secret, as though she already knew what storms lay ahead.

Chapter 17 – The Pact of Teeth

Flashback — The Visitors Rain woke in the night to find the walls trembling with strange light. Not fire. Not moonlight. Something softer, as if the air itself had turned translucent. Shapes stirred where shadows should have been —tall, blurred at the edges, presence more felt than seen. Her parents rushed to her bedside, shielding her though they didn't know from what. Panic filled the small house. The shapes only hovered. They did not cross fully into the room. Rain felt no fear. Only a strange calm, as though some part of her had always known them. A whisper pressed itself into her skull: "The bridge must endure." Her parents clutched her tighter. But Rain only tilted her head, listening. It was the first time the Inol revealed themselves —

though no one would ever truly understand why they had chosen her.

The Fortune's Hold The Wolf sank deeper into the Fortune's ribbed throat. Red lamps swung like lanterns in a wind that wasn't there. Chains groaned overhead. Crew eyes followed from the rigging, sharp as knives and twice as patient. Faber and Mereya stepped onto the deck, every motion taut with suspicion.

Schrödinger stood waiting, coat draped like a banner, ruined symmetry stranger under the scarlet glow. Pippin loomed beside him, one ear cut to a stump, grin crooked and unreadable. "These faces," Schrödinger said, spreading his hand toward the watching crew, "are why this vessel sails at all. Every scar on her ribs, every mast still upright — paid for in their blood, not mine." His hand fell

heavy on Pippin's shoulder. "And this one most of all. He's bled for me more than once. I'd be ash without him." The crew leaned forward slightly, proud of their scars, proud of their captain's words. Faber ignored the theater. His eyes measured exits, bulkheads, the cable coiled near the hatch. Mereya tightened her grip on the containment cradle.

Teeth and Storms
Schrödinger's gaze slid inevitably to the cradle. His tone softened into something like reverence. "Funny thing about doors," he murmured. "You never know which side you're on. Open the wrong one —you're prey. Open the right one —you're king. I've opened enough to learn neither side lasts." Faber's voice was flat. "And you think this one makes you king?" "Not me." Schrödinger's ruined smile bared a hint of fang.

"I'm not greedy enough to touch it twice.
But I'd be a fool not to sail with those carrying it.
Storms follow such cargo.
And storms are where legends are written." "Legends don't shield flesh,"

Mereya snapped. Schrödinger's tail flicked lazily. "True. But neither does hiding. South of here, the world respects only teeth." "Teeth break," Faber said. "Ah," Schrödinger countered, voice dropping low, "but storms remember who dared to bite at all." The silence thickened until —

Rain's Voice "All this talk of doors and debts," came Rain's voice, airy, childlike. "Dull. If you're going to scare them, Schrödinger, tell a story that doesn't creak." Chains above clinked once, then stilled. Crew eyes darted to the cradle. Schrödinger leaned closer, his ruined face lit by the red lamps. "A child's tongue with an old

echo in it," he murmured. "I wonder who fears it more —my crew… or you." Rain's giggle was sly. "Maybe both. Maybe neither." Faber's hand twitched near his belt. Mereya caught the motion, steadying him with a look. Her voice cut through the air, calm and sharp. "This doesn't change what we came for. Passage south. Nothing more." Schrödinger straightened, coat flaring like smoke in a storm wind. His smile turned crooked again. "And nothing less. Very well. Let teeth and tide test us all." Pippin barked a laugh, swinging up into the rigging. "Rig the nets! Bring her in!" Chains strained as the Fortune drew the Wolf deeper into its cavernous hold. Shadows folded over steel. The two ships became one silhouette stitched by canvas and chain. Faber's jaw locked.

Mereya's grip held tight. And from the cradle, Rain hummed to herself —a tune soft as a lullaby, sharp as glass. Not laughter this time, but patience.

As though she already knew what storms lay ahead.

Chapter 18 – The Green Veil


Flashback — Carried Away Rain dreamt her room
was no longer hers. The walls breathed like lungs,
stretching and folding as if the space itself were alive.
She drifted through corridors that opened and closed
like gills. The Inol never spoke with mouths, but their
presence pressed words into her bones: oceans drying,
forests burning, skies turning to ash. In her chest, a
light —seedlike, pulsing. They showed her what she
was, though she didn't understand. Not yet. When she
reached for her parents, they were already fading,
voices swallowed by the walls. The Inol didn't
explain.
They only carried her forward.

The Green Horizon The Fortune and the Wolf moved
south together, bound by chains

and shadow. Below stretched the wreck of continents:
mountains drowned in forests, cities smothered under
centuries of dust, rivers that no longer obeyed
their names. Behind them, the Republic's lattice
dimmed. Ahead, silence grew heavier with every
mile. Then the world turned green. At first, it looked
like canopy. But as the Fortune dropped lower, it
revealed itself for what it was: not trees.
Not vines. Not anything that should have endured.
Kudzu. Not the weed that once climbed fences and

barns. Its nightmare twin —magnified until each coil was thick as towers, each tendril stretching miles. It moved without wind, curling and recoiling like thought itself. Mereya gripped the railing, knuckles white. "It's… alive." Faber said nothing. He only felt the Fortune shudder, as though

even machines knew what loomed below. Schrödinger's ears twitched. His voice held no amusement. "That is no growth. That is the Kudzu Field. And somewhere beneath it waits your door." The silence on the deck grew heavy, as if even sound hesitated.

The Pause — The Toad of Kudzu The veil was endless. Green. Alive. And the story stirred. Long ago, when the Soul of the World still anchored life, balance held. But when the Moon fractured and Earth burned, a shadow seeped into soil, into marrow, into roots. That shadow clothed itself in vines. It multiplied until the world itself recoiled. Kudzu, once harmless, became the mouth of hatred. And hatred grew a body. A toad. Not born, but swollen. Not grown, but gathered. Hatred clothed in skin. Its warts were scars —each lump a war never forgiven. Its eyes were ponds reflecting only the worst of what leaned

over them. The vines were its breath. Its hymn. Its prison. Where the Soul whispered patience to the ferrets, the Toad croaked only hunger: to choke, devour, unmake. Some called it the Soul's shadow. Others, its rival. But the truth was crueler: it was the Soul's reflection. The part that could not forgive. One truth endured: What grows from love endures. What grows from hate devours.

Back on Deck The deck creaked again —crew shifting, chains rattling. Mereya's hand brushed the cradle instinctively. Faber's palm was slick against the rail. Schrödinger lit a long stemmed pipe, smoke curling slow around his ruined face.
"Now you see why teeth won't carry you through. That field doesn't choke just forests.

It chokes memory. Reason. Courage." From the cradle came Rain's voice — bright, sly: "Then it's good you brought me. Vines don't like fire." Her giggle spilled across the deck, wrong for the weight of the moment. Even
Schrödinger's smile faltered.

Chapter 19 – Veinwork


Flashback: The Bargain Rain sat on her mother's lap, a sweater sleeve bunched in her
fists, while the living room bent at the edges like heat above asphalt. The lights didn't flicker —light itself seemed to hold its breath. Shapes gathered in the corners, not quite touching the floor or walls, as if the room were a map and they were the cartographer's hand above it. Her father stood
with a wrench he had no use for, jaw clenched so hard his temples throbbed. A voice —not heard, but understood —filled the air like a tide rising. The bridge must endure or all the cycles end. The words came without mouths. The shapes did not blink. Her mother shook

her head until the motion dissolved into sobs. Her father took one step forward, then another, each smaller than the last.
The shapes let him run out of courage. They showed the three of them a future like a pane of glass: sky shattered to gravel, seas forgetting their names, a seed glowing behind Rain's ribs. Preserve her. Mind and map.
Flesh when the world can carry it again. Her mother pressed her cheek to Rain's hair and whispered, "We will find you," to the child, the shapes, and no one at

all. Her father lowered the wrench. He didn't drop it; he set it down carefully, as if that choice mattered. Then he nodded into the air and said the smallest word a man can say. "Please."

Into the Green Veil They left the Republic's edge at first light —the kind of light that looked like freshly sanded steel—moving in a

staggered column along the old relief road until the road ended and something else began. The Green Veil had been only color at a distance. Up close it was sound. Kudzu hummed. Not with bees or wind, but with arithmetic —tendrils counting, leaves tabulating, stems dividing the world into agreeable and not. The Deceitful Fortune had set down inland the night before on a basalt shelf, masts braced against a sky that occasionally threw pebbles of moonfire at the Republic's shields far north. Schrödinger's crew fanned out, cat -quiet even when they weren't cats: Nix and Wicket in patched cuirasses, wiry post -human riggers, foxes moving like knives told as jokes. Pippin ghosted point, carbine snug, his one -eared silhouette iconic as a banner. Faber checked his kit: gray -pistol under the jacket, knife at his kidney, microline

spool at his hip.
The med -seal across his ribs tugged when he breathed too deep. He counted that tug among the things keeping him honest. "On foot from here," Mereya said, visor painting faint blue hazard glyphs

across her vision. "The Fortune can't push air this thick without setting herself on fire." "Feels like she'd enjoy that," Faber muttered. Schrödinger smiled without showing teeth. "She would. But I'd like to keep my reputation attached to something steerable." Rain's voice rang out from the cradle, bright as a bell in an empty hall. "The door is ahead. Not a door-door. A mouth that forgot how to bite." Pippin glanced back. "Comforting," he said. "Always wanted to be swallowed politely." "Stay polite on my deck and the world swallows slower," Schrödinger said. Then, to Faber: "We

take your lead. You brought the compass." Faber didn't look at the cube at Mereya's side. He looked at her instead. "Hear that? We're the compass." "We," she agreed, letting her shoulder touch his. A promise small enough to travel. They stepped into the Veil.

Inside the Veil Beneath the first arch of Kudzu the air cooled by a degree you could feel in your molars. Sunlight filtered down in narrow columns like cathedral dust. The ground had been road once; now it was a rumor under soft green.
The crew moved without chatter. Even Nix and Wicket sobered under that shade. "Left," Rain directed. "Then left again. Then stop, because the ground only pretends to keep going." They followed her word. Ten meters on, the "ground" revealed itself —lattice grown

over a drainage cut, a green drumhead stretched above black. "Would have held a cat. Maybe," Pippin muttered. "Which is why you don't test with cats," Schrödinger replied. They laid the first line. Faber anchored it

to fused vine and brick; Mereya checked the tension with her usual impatience. They moved like climbers inside a throat, stepping from lamppost bones to Kudzu bridges.

Ahead, a false façade appeared: windows framed in leaves, doorway curtained in vine, and in that doorway two slow gleams like coins in deep water. Not eyes —seed pods polished until they reflected whatever stared. "Pretty," Rain said. "Don't let it sing." "It sings?" Pippin whispered. "It would if it could." They eased past, unease settling into the familiar shape of caution.

The Mouth

They reached the first Kollosol marker: a gear enclosing a triple helix, bubbled with age and scarred by acid. The past was a hard meal. Mereya crouched near the stamp. "South branch facility. Auxiliary systems. Emergency ingress." "Enough remains," Schrödinger said. Crates lay half -buried beyond, stenciled KOLLOSOL —BIO-FRAME — FRAGILE. The vowels weathered away. "They left in a hurry," Pippin said. "Everyone did," Faber answered. The Kudzu shifted as they pressed deeper. Twice Rain stopped them a heartbeat before thorns lifted like glass. Once she urged them to hurry through air thick as honey. They obeyed. The road dropped into a bowl where Kudzu had woven itself into purpose. At the center lay a circle of concrete five meters across, six petals around a

cracked control core. "The mouth," Rain said. "It forgot how to bite." Mereya knelt, tools in hand. The panel flickered faintly under her shadow. "Old biometric mesh," she muttered. "Director clearance. And… something else.
Less human."
"Inol?" Schrödinger asked. "Or the myth of them," Faber said. Rain hummed.
"Not a trick. A toy. It only opens if you've been told you're allowed." "Are you allowed?" Pippin asked. "I can say hello," she replied.
"I can't say goodnight." They exchanged a glance. Try a soft probe. Don't trigger it hard. If it purrs, step back. If it growls, run. Mereya lowered the Ciliax cradle onto the bowl's rim. Its seams glowed faintly.

Rain whispered: "Hello." Light threaded the cracks. Kudzu rustled overhead. The ground shifted like a sleeper turning in bed. A sharp sweetness filled the air, metallic as blood. "Enough," Mereya warned, pulling back. The glow faded reluctantly. Pippin returned from the perimeter, whiskers wet with dew. "Warm door," he said. "But something big made a path here last night. Don't want to be the third trail." Rain's voice grew quiet. "It hears us." "Then we camp," Schrödinger ordered.

## Camp

They set bivouacs under the canopy. Watches in pairs. No fires. Faber patrolled the rim of the bowl. Beneath leaf -litter he found a vent: steel grille, helix stamped in concrete, moss furred. Root hairs probed the air, recoiled at his touch. "Curious," he murmured.

"Hungry," Rain corrected. Mereya joined him, visor up, bare to the humid air. "I hate that I can smell the building," she said. "Like a hospital pretending to be a forest." He took her hand. For a moment, pulse steadied breath. Night thickened. The ground spoke —a pressure wave large enough to persuade bone. The petals flexed inward, then out. Pippin hissed: "North trench. Movement. Not us." Scrapes. Then silence. Waiting. "Tomorrow," Faber whispered. "We open it tomorrow." "Together," Mereya said, shoulder against his. The Veil resumed its arithmetic. Rain whispered a word that might have been soon. They slept the way soldiers do —piecemeal, suspicious, close to the thing that would demand their story at

first light.

Chapter 20 – Cathedral of Rot

Flashback: The Goodbye The house was small, the world outside smaller still. The sky burned with falling stone, thunder that wasn't weather. Inside, the night was only lanternlight and grief. Rain's parents sat with her in the corner of the single room, holding her between them as if their arms alone might defy the universe. Her mother pressed frantic kisses into Rain's hair. Stay. Please stay. Just stay. Her father clenched his fists into his own flesh, as if pain could undo a choice already made. At the center of the room waited the Ciliax chamber: pale alloy folded into the shape of a coffin designed for dreams. It hummed faintly, unbearably. Rain had cried until tears emptied themselves. Now her wide eyes searched her parents' faces, waiting for

an explanation. A low growl came from the doorway. Locke, the family's dog, hackles up, tail stiff. He didn't understand the device, but he understood loss, and it was wrong. He circled, whining once, daring the world to come through him first. Her father tried to smile. It broke halfway. "You'll sleep," he said softly. "Just for a little while. When you wake, the world will be better." Her mother's tears wet Rain's cheeks. "Don't promise that," she whispered. "We don't know. We don't know anything." But they knew one thing: they couldn't

stop it. Together, trembling, they lifted Rain. She reached for them even as the chamber closed, palms pressed against the glass until their shapes blurred. Her mother laid her own hand to the barrier. Her father whispered her name like a

prayer no god was listening to. The chamber sealed. The hum deepened. A glow spread through its alloy like a heartbeat that no longer belonged to her. Her mother collapsed against it, clutching as if sheer force could pry it open again. Her father fell to his knees. Locke barked once, furious, then lay pressed against the machine's base, vowing never to leave her side. Rain's tiny hand slid down the inside of the glass, then stilled. The goodbye was not ceremony. It was the sound of a family breaking.

Descent into the Cathedral The storm line broke, revealing the wreck of the southern plain. Kudzu made hills of buildings, waves of roads, a mouth of earth that smiled. "The line ends here," Faber murmured. They'd come on foot from the last skiff landing. The Deceitful Fortune waited at the ridge with a skeleton crew to guard

retreat. Air tasted of iron and sap. Wind whispered in the vines like a crowd trying to stay polite. Rusted signage jutted up from the green like bones of an alphabet no one used anymore. Mereya adjusted the cradle's strap, the Ciliax's weight obscene in its

smallness. "We keep it sealed," she said. "No connections. No tests. Don't feed anything that hums." "Seconded," Schrödinger said. His coat hung heavy with oil slick damp. His uneven eyes refused to agree on what they saw, yet missed nothing. "And keep skin covered.
If the Kudzu touches, it remembers."
Pippin padded alongside him, coil -thrower slung, hook -knife at his thigh. Merri ghosted behind — smaller, silent, shadow -sharp. Cats, Nix and Wicket, and two wiry dogs trailed on tether -lines like divers under hostile seas. "You're stepping wrong," Rain said from the

cradle, her voice bright as a coin dropped down a dry well. "Explain,"
Mereya said. "The ground used to go down there," Rain answered, tone too casual, pointing them toward a collapsed highway now smothered in
green. "And the air tastes like melted batteries. Bad for lungs. Good for maps." Faber touched the wolf -tooth charm he wore when numbers felt too thin. "You can taste maps now?" "I can taste everything," Rain said. "It's noisy here. Like standing beside a river of fingerprints." The Kudzu rose in curtains and vaults, architecture grown out of appetite. Transmission towers became reeds in a wind that blew from nowhere. Leaves thickened into surfaces you could read by touch. The plant brushed their

suits with a softness that made Fabers skin crawl beneath the fabric. "See how it pulses?" Mereya whispered. "Not just with wind." He did. The Kudzu moved like an animal deciding which way to turn. Schrödinger lifted a paw. "Hear that?" Pippin frowned. "I hear everything." "Exactly," Schrödinger murmured. "None of it's birds."

## The Cathedral Wakes

The vines shuddered. The floor flexed, then smoothed like a sheet drawing breath. A valley opened. Not collapse —decision. Kudzu drew back in ripples, revealing a nave: a long green aisle floored in woven stems, walls ribbed with roots, a ceiling hammered into stained glass by the sun. At the far end rose the facility, Kollosol concrete intact beneath the garden that ate cities.

"Cathedral," Merri whispered. "A cathedral of rot." "Hold your metaphors," Schrödinger said, though even his voice softened. "I feel very welcome," Rain murmured. "No," Mereya snapped, to the cradle. "Not yet." They advanced down the aisle. Silence thickened until even their breath felt trespass. Then the Kudzu sang. Not sound — pressure. A note sustained in their bones. Vines uncurled, thickened, knotted with pulsing nodes. From beneath, something knocked. The Toad emerged. First mound, then mouth, then limb. A vast blunt head crowned with moss, eyes like church

windows, a mouth wide enough to show a city's teeth.
Kudzu cradled it like a throne.
The cathedral breathed with it. They ran.
The Toad cut them off by being. Tendrils

braided ahead, lattice closing like a book. They hurled
brittle charges, vines crisping to glass for heartbeats.
Faber's knife cut, Mereya's coilgun thundered,
Schrödinger swore in a storm's language.
Above, the ceiling opened to sunlight around the
Toad's head, a grotesque halo. Schrödinger stopped.
He measured risk against legend, and chose the latter.
He lifted his blade in invitation. "Take me. Not
them." "Captain, no!" Pippin's voice broke. The Toad
struck. A tendril punched through Schrödinger's
chest, lifting him like a doll, then letting him fall.
Pippin made a sound Faber had never heard from
the living. He dragged his captain clear, fury burning
into ritual. Merri's coil cut daylight along the
monster's lip. "Back!"

Faber snapped, placing himself between the Toad and
everything else. Rain's hum lashed the air. Vines
recoiled. The facility's sealed seam glowed faintly, as
if remembering its name. The Toad hesitated.
Recognition, not fear. It lowered its head, studying.
Then, with a sigh like a delta meeting sea, it sank
back into its cathedral. Silence, save for the sounds of
the living hurting. Pippin knelt, blood and salt and
iron in his hands. He opened the ritual kit. His voice
steadied. "Blood to blood, name to name. Come back,

Captain. Come back." The world did not change —
until it did. Schrödinger gasped, rude and alive.
"See?" he rasped. "Leaving always costs." "Breathing
does too," Pippin growled, furious with relief. Rain
giggled softly. "I wasn't shouting. I was humming.
Your

ears are just bad." "Only one," Pippin muttered, and
the cradle chimed with laughter. Faber turned to the
door.
Frost traced its face like constellations learning to
spell. "Rain," Mereya whispered. "Can you knock?"
"I can do better," she said, and the
facility stirred. The door did not open. But it admitted
the idea of opening. For now, that was victory
enough.

85


Part 3: Ashes

Chapter 21 – The Second Hymn
They carried the captain back like contraband, wrapped in coats and silence. The Deceitful Fortune opened her belly to receive him. Red lamps swung in the docking throat. The galleon creaked as if in sympathy. Pippin never once looked away from Schrödinger's face, not even to check his footing. Merri kept a hand steadying the first mate's back, silent. On deck, the air felt clean only because it smelled of oil and iron instead of sap. Someone had laid canvas over a crate for a table. Someone else had already set boiled water and needles that had lived too many lives. Faber stood off to the side, his knife hand empty, the fresh wound high on his arm bandaged but throbbing like a second

pulse. "Set him," Pippin said, voice gravel. They obeyed him like breath. Schrödinger lay pale beneath the ruin of his symmetry, lips salted by ritual. Still, he smiled the stubborn smile. "Next time," he rasped, "I'll let the beast take my bad side." "You don't have one," Pippin growled, packing cloth against the wound. Mereya hovered over Faber a moment too long. Her fingers touched his forearm —light, exact, the old message: I see what you're not saying. Come back. He nodded once. Rain was quiet in the cradle, which for her meant only that she let the ship's noise move unremarked. Faber still felt her attention, heavy as a child's gaze in a room where adults whispered lies. The argument began as inventory. "We've got six chorus

charges," Merri said, laying the fat cylinders out. "Two are partial. I can retune them to the note she hummed at the door. But we'll need more." "Can you make more?" Mereya asked. "If I strip three coil housings and the forward speaker guts," Merri said. "And your coilgun." Mereya unbuckled it without ceremony. "Take what sings." Faber exhaled. The air tasted of relief, and relief was a
trap. "We hit the door again at night. Less heat, less motion. Charges light, blades clean. No standing where the floor can choose." Schrödinger coughed a laugh, winced. "Bring a better hymn," he added. "One note won't do. We need a chord." Pippin looked up from the work with the face Faber trusted most — love burned down to steel. "We're short hands," he said. "Not short anger. I'll

make anger grip a tool." The deck speakers hissed, then spat static down the rigging like rain. A voice clawed its way out: "…Echelon Blue, do you copy? This is Lion Gate. Multiple breaches —outer ring compromised along the rail. Arc Net live for debris, but the Crown is inside. Repeat: inside. Civilians to vaults, reserves to the stone roads. Baron unit is — " static broke the word into a fall, then returned, higher, terrified. "If anyone's in range —if anyone —we need…" The deck froze.
Even the lamps stopped swinging.
Merri's hands stalled over a charge. Pippin stopped breathing. Faber's spine turned to wire. Schrödinger closed his eyes. When he opened them, command

sat there, cruel and clear. "Kill the line," he said softly. "Captain —" Merri began. "Kill it," he repeated. "Before it makes

cowards of us." No one moved. Rain did it instead, thinning the static to a thread:
"…the
Crown's on the steps. They're chanting.
They —" The line died with a pop. Silence, except for Faber's pulse. "What were they chanting?" Merri whispered. Rain answered, bright as fact. "Witness me, mirror me, same frame, god of the machine."
"Crown rubbish," Pippin spat. Faber stared into the hatchway, seeing not corridors but debts. Part of him wanted to bolt for the pilot's chair. The rest knew the math. Leave now and the door closes forever.
Mereya's voice cut sharp. "If the Republic burns, it burns without us. But if we fail here, there will be nothing left worth saving." The words stung because they were true.

Work as Mercy They fell into it. Merri stripped coils, retuned charges. Rain hummed

notes into their guts until they clicked like purring throats. One note made the door listen.
Another made the Kudzu flinch.
Together, they would carve a path.
Schrödinger tried to stand; Pippin shoved him down. Faber claimed point. "You'll come, Captain. But you won't lead. That's mine." Mereya approved with a glance sharp as steel. "Point keeps changing," she

said. Rain sang again, small and perfect. The frost -
lines on the door miles away seemed to answer in
memory.

Closing Image

They stood at the hatch, packs humming with
charges, blades sharp, rifles loaded.
Behind them, the Republic screamed. Ahead, the
Kudzu swayed like a congregation waiting for its next
hymn. Faber's hand brushed Mereya's arm. She
tapped back: Come back. Rain giggled in

the cradle, pleased. "The door's listening again," she
said. "Then let's make it open," Faber answered, and
they stepped into the green.

## Chapter 22 – The Door That Hums

The door loomed, silent as a cliff face. Kudzu wrapped it like a gift to no one, vines threaded into seams, leaves pressed flat as if listening through metal. It wasn't just shut —it was waiting. The landing party stood in its shadow, exhaustion written in the small ways: Schrödinger leaning heavy on Pippin, Merri crouched with eyes on the rhythm of vines, even Nix and
Wicket subdued, whiskers twitching like antennae. Faber stared at the sealed alloy. He'd looked down warlords, assassins, void storms. None of them looked back the way this thing did. "It's aware," Mereya said. Her palm rested against the seam. The cradle on her chest thrummed, its vibration carrying into her bones. "Not alive. Aware."

"Facilities don't get to be aware," Faber muttered. "Then explain that." Schrödinger lifted one crooked finger toward the vines. They shifted, subtle but unmistakable, curling tighter around the frame as though
defending territory. "It remembers footsteps. That's why the plant hasn't swallowed this place. I t's guarding something." Rain's voice rang from the cradle, bright and calm: "The door doesn't like you." Faber turned sharply. "It doesn't like any of us."

"No," Rain said. "But it likes me." The words landed like frost across the crew.

Faber's Rifle

The silence thickened. Kudzu stirred without wind. Faber's jaw clenched. He knelt, snapping open the old satchel from Titan. Inside lay the scavenger's coil rifle —ugly, brutal, patched from centuries -old parts:

Republic stock, pirate barrel, plating scorched with use. Its power cell sat strapped in with leather that smelled of blood. He lifted it with both hands, checking welds by habit. Capacitors whined awake, the weapon growling like a predator pulled from sleep. Schrödinger cocked his head, uneven eyes gleaming. "Since when do you play long gun, collector?" "Since knives stopped being enough," Faber said flatly. He braced, sighted, and fired. The rifle roared, a bolt of coiled light punching through Kudzu. Sap hissed into steam, vines writhed, and for one clean instant they saw the door bare —its alloy skin smooth, patient, unbroken. The Kudzu shrieked. Not sound but pressure, a weight on their chests, their teeth,
their thoughts. Rain cut through it like a bell. "That was loud. Too loud. The door

heard you." "Good," Faber growled, snapping the reload. "Let it know we're knocking."

The Listening Green

They advanced cautiously. Vines knitted back almost immediately, eager to erase the wound Faber had made. They didn't strike —they flexed, deliberate, curious. Mereya lifted the cradle higher, coil pistol drawn in her other hand. Her eyes never left the green. "Rain. You said it likes you. Show me." Rain giggled once, then softened into resonance —not words but vibration, low and patient. The cradle pulsed in unison, glowing faintly. The vines bowed. Some recoiled. And the door shivered. Frost etched its face in spreading lines, geometry blooming like constellations. The crew froze. "She's singing to it," Merri whispered. Faber kept the rifle steady, even as awe crawled cold along his spine. "Then let it sing back."

The Door That Hums

The pattern deepened. The alloy itself began to vibrate, humming low, a sound that lived in bone. Stone grinding. Mountains shifting. A vault remembering its purpose.
Schrödinger gave a ragged laugh. "Of course Kollosol built doors that sing." "Not singing," Rain corrected, eerily patient. "Listening." The vines bowed lower, the whole cathedral leaning in. Faber's grip tightened on the rifle. Every instinct screamed that silence could turn to violence in a blink. The hum rose. Frost light converged into a circle at the seam's center. Not

opening, not yet — only admitting the idea of opening. Mereya's heart thudded hard. "Rain. Stop if it hurts you." "It doesn't hurt," Rain whispered, dreamy. "It feels… familiar."

Shadows of the Crown

The hum filled the nave. Then static crackled. A battered radio on one raccoon's back coughed into life: "… Crown forces in the Republic capital… breach through western gate… civilians sheltering… defenses strained…" The voice warped, clipped, then returned raw and terrified: "They're chanting as they kill — witness me, mirror me, same frame, god of the machine —" Silence. Merri swore. Schrödinger's ears flattened. Faber did not lower the rifle. "Focus. We finish this first. Then we deal with them." Rain's hum faltered, then steadied. "They're loud too. But not here. Not yet." The frost -light dimmed, heartbeat fading back into sleep. The hum lingered — waiting. Faber clenched his jaw. They had touched it, but not enough.
Closing Image

The Kudzu swayed like a congregation in silence.

The door glowed faintly, riddle half finished. Faber stood with rifle hot in his hands. Mereya clutched the cradle as if it might break or save them. Schrödinger leaned heavy against Pippin. Merri's eyes stayed sharp.

And Rain sang softly to something that had waited centuries to hear her voice. The door did not open. But it had listened.
And in a world that had forgotten how to listen, that was enough —for now.

Chapter 23 – Echoes in the Green

The hum lingered long after the door fell silent. Faber felt it under his ribs, a resonance like the echo of thunder, unwilling to leave. The frost -lines across the alloy still glowed faintly, like constellations remembered only in fragments. The facility had listened. That was worse than if it had ignored them. They retreated to the Deceitful Fortune, but rest was a fiction. Kudzu pressed against the ship's hull, roots burrowing into seams, vines curling over plating. Every creak of timber became a threat. Every breath tasted of sap, sharp as rusted iron. The green did not sleep. It only waited. Merri crouched in the corner of the mess, her coilwork spread like a surgeon's table. Chorus charges lay gleaming, brass throats pulsing

faintly as she teased their innards alive. Each throb made the deck tremble. Rain giggled from the cradle, bright as broken glass. "It tickles," she said. Beneath the laughter, something weightier stirred — an eagerness that didn't belong to a child. Pippin ignored her. His hands worked silently over Schrödinger's wounds, rewrapping chest and ribs with patience sharpened into anger. The captain smiled anyway, thin and stubborn. "If I fall again," he rasped, "drag me feet -first. Makes for a longer story ." "You'll walk," Pippin growled, tying the knot harder than he needed. "One way or another." Mereya stood by the hatch, arms folded, eyes fixed on the slit where Kudzu scraped the hull. She had hardly spoken since the door hummed. Faber joined her without asking, rifle across his back, listening

with her to the faint rasp of vine on metal.
The silence broke with static. The battered radio strapped to a raccoon's back coughed into life: "… breach… Crown banners inside… civilians forced to vaults…" The voice clipped, then returned high and raw: "They're chanting even as they kill — witness me, mirror me, same frame, god of the machine —"
Silence. Merri swore.
Schrödinger's uneven eyes narrowed.
"The Republic bleeds," he said softly.
Pippin's fists shook.
"Then we should be there." "No," Faber snapped.
"We go now, we lose everything. The door closes.

Rain stays where she is. The Crown wins twice."
Mereya's voice cut clean as glass: "If the Republic falls, it burns without us. If we fail here —if she fails here —there won't be a world worth saving." The weight of her words crushed the room into silence.

The Kudzu Sings

That night, the Kudzu began to sing. Not attack — sing. The vines against the hull scraped into rhythm. The timbers groaned in pitch. The air in the corridors carried faint resonance, a mimicry of Rain's hum.

Faber woke with the rifle in hand. He found Merri already awake, coilgun across her knees. "It's listening," she whispered. "It's practicing." The thought settled like cold iron. The Kudzu was adapting.

Return to the Nave

At dawn—or what passed for dawn beneath bruised skies

—they returned. The vines parted without resistance. Not violence, not force. They ushered the crew in, weaving aside like polite hosts. It was worse than ambush. They advanced tethered by black cord, every step deliberate. Schrödinger leaned against Pippin, pale but upright. Merri counted the rhythm of vines under her breath. Nix and Wicket ghosted ahead, whiskers trembling. The door loomed. Frost -lines faint but undeniable. Waiting. Rain stirred in the cradle, her voice dream -heavy. "It wants to see me." Faber's hand tightened on the rifle. "Then it can earn the privilege." Merri set a chorus charge at the nave's center. Its tone scraped the vines raw; they recoiled. Mereya lifted the cradle higher. "Rain," she said softly. The child hummed. The frost flared, constellations blooming into sharper patterns. Faber felt it in his teeth, in his bones.

Schrödinger's uneven gaze sharpened.
"Closer," he rasped. "Closer than last time."
The Kudzu bowed low, cathedral trembling as

though inside a vast lung. Faber braced the
rifle.
"Then let's make it open." The door
hummed back. Not surrender. Not refusal.
Acknowledgment. A vibration too deep for
ears, spiraling into bone. The frost -light
blazed, forming a circle at the seam's
heart. Twice it pulsed
—like a heartbeat answering Rain's song.
The
Kudzu swayed as one, a congregation
bowing in silence. The facility was waking.

## Chapter 24 – Hollow Gods

The seam in the door quivered, tasting the air like a tongue. Rain's note fell away, and frost -lines flared, slid, and sighed open. The Kudzu withdrew in inches, reluctant as curtains torn from a window. "Forward," Faber said. They entered as they had sworn — tethered, measured, no heroics. Merri cradled a chorus charge ready to sing; Faber took point, rifle low. Mereya carried the cradle high, hands free. Schrödinger leaned harder than he admitted on Pippin, the first mate's knot s tugging him upright. Nix and Wicket ghosted flank, whiskers twitching. Inside smelled of cold metal and old light. Darkness swallowed them first, the kind that makes you count your teeth. Then filaments buzzed alive, one by one, an

uncertain constellation. Their glow seemed to pulse in time with the hum Rain had left behind. The corridor was too tall, its surfaces poured instead of built. Symbols ran ankle high along the walls, delicate geometrics that twitched when stared at. Kudzu had found the seams, threading them like veins, writing in hunger. They turned a corner —and found the pods. Glass coffers lined the walls, thirty or more. Most were milked with frost, figures blurred inside. Some held only vines pressed to throats and temples like lovers. Others showed pale arms, curled knees, half -faces webbed in green. The Kudzu was not eating them. It was sharing. "It's interfacing," Merri whispered. "System to system." "Or the system is interfacing with it," Faber said grimly. Rain hummed. The nearest pod

brightened, pale shape within turning as though to listen.
Mereya snapped her head down. "Stop." "I didn't touch," Rain said.
"They're tired." Faber pressed his palm flat to glass until the hum broke. "Not now." They moved on.

The Hollow Chamber

The corridor opened into vastness. Columns curved like ribs. Machines rose like organs, spiraled and latticed, pulsing faintly. Catwalks stitched the space like thoughts too thin to trust. Kudzu climbed with unsettling grace, draping instead of choking, leaves glowing faintly where they drank alloy's charge.
"They look like gods left hollow," Pippin murmured.
"Or the idea of gods," Schrödinger rasped.
"Something to kneel to." Faber

swept his rifle, math grounding him: angles, cover, exits. Rain hummed again. Lights stirred. Relays clicked.
Pumps sighed like old men considering duty. Frost brightened across one ribbed column, patterns whispering of bridges and debts. The raccoon's radio

hissed alive: "… breach contained… Crown fragments inside… citizens shelter —" The voice clipped into squeal. Silence followed. Faber's jaw hardened. "We finish this. Then we run." They found a stair bolted to a column. Fab er tested the first step. It held. They climbed, shadows stretching thin. A catwalk delivered them to another seam. Frost traced it faintly, waiting. "Again?" Mereya asked. "Again," Rain answered, delighted. She hummed fine as wire. The seam's circle bloomed small, glowing like a lock waiting for its song. "Not

enough," Rain whispered. "It wants… the other piece. The one shaped like me." A silence deeper than fear pressed against them. Faber lowered his rifle a hair, pointed down a shadowed catwalk.
"Then we keep going." Merri swallowed. "Careful," she muttered. They edged along, the chamber's hollow gods watching in silence. Behind them, the Kudzu shivered once, passing a message by touch. And was still.

## Chapter 25 — The Symbioses Maw

The corridor narrowed and then forgot how to be a corridor. Concrete rippled into ribs. Conduits braided with vine. Emergency strips that should have glowed white instead pulsed a patient green, like veins showing off under skin. Somewhere behind the walls , pumps sighed — wet, satisfied. "Older warning glyphs here," Merri said, sweeping her hand -lamp across a collapsed sign. Letters peeled up under the light, bleeding from yellow to bone: BIOLOGICAL FUSION / DO NOT INTERFACE. Pippin snorted. "Bit late." Faber checked the scavenger rifle's cell again out of habit. The capacitors purred awake, eager as dogs at a door. He preferred

the knife for truth's sake, but the facility had made knives feel too small. Rain hummed low in the cradle against Mereya's chest, careful, careful. "Same song," she whispered, not to them but to the walls. "Different throats." "The Toad," Schrödinger rasped, leaning too heavily on Pippin to hide the tremor in his stride. "Its pulse is in the plumbing." "Means the plant's wired to the core," Merri said. "If it panics, the walls turn into a lung." "Then don't panic it," Faber said.
The first husker came out of the wall like a bad memory made to walk. It had been a man once.

Features sagged and webbed, vines scaffolding the spine and jaw, eyes filmed white but watching for the Kudzu.
Another husk followed, dragging the rusted shell of a drone like a pet toy.
Rain whispered, "Don't kill them.

They're echoes. Puppets. The people are gone." Faber didn't argue. "Echoes still cut. Down one knee." The rifle cracked, coil-bolt hissing sap into steam. Mereya's compact pistol stitched two cords that lunged for Faber. Pippin hooked low, taking the legs out from under another husk. Merri tossed a brittle charge, the pop turning vines brittle enough to smash under boots. Schrödinger's pulse pistol burned a line near the drone's head, and Pippin finished it with a quick, surgical twist.
Silence fell again, embarrassed. "Echoes," Pippin muttered. "We'll honor what they were by not letting them make more." Rain said nothing. Mereya felt the cradle's hum steady against her ribs.

The gallery broke into an atrium —and into something more. Columns bulged like ribs.
Machinery had become organs, draped in Kudzu that glowed faintly

where leaf touched alloy. In the center swelled a knot: cables and vines braided into one body, pulsing green -white like a heart. Faces formed in its weave, un - formed, and formed again. Merri swore softly. "That shouldn't be alive." "It isn't," Rain said, then contradicted herself: "It is." The knot pulsed harder, and the ceiling sagged as if to fold the chamber into its mouth. "Chorus one," Merri snapped, rolling the cylinder into the swell.

The note it sang bent the air, made vines twitch. The floor stuttered flat. "Key!" she barked. Mereya lifted the cradle. Rain hummed. A catwalk extended further into the atrium, metal finding memory. They had a path. The Kudzu didn't let them go politely. Tendrils came in ropes and nets, thick with the suggestion of hands. Faber fired. Mereya

burned.

Pippin's bloodied knife drew a warding circle. Schrödinger, pale and furious, carved where the vines pressed closest. "Bridge ahead!" Merri called. They ran, boots hammering, cutting where the floor sagged. Mid span, a tendril wrapped the bridge from below, dragging it into a tongue. Pippin's coil -thrower stuttered a line of bolts; the plant recoiled, furious. But a knot let lunged from the side and bit Schrödinger across the ribs. He didn't scream. He just locked eyes with Pippin, jaw iron, until Pippin's blade forced the vine to spit him out. They staggered the last steps, dragging him onto the far platform. Ahead: a service door filigreed in vines, as if the plant had spent years practicing its calligraphy. Merri slapped a brittle charge against the seam. The

vines hissed brittle and snapped. The door groaned open.  Cold air exhaled. Clean. Mineral. Not plant - breath. The chamber beyond yawned like a throat of light, seven decks deep, its walls lined with pods stacked in a transparent alloy. Frost glimmered at their seams. Some were empty. Some were occupied. Not all shapes inside were human. Not all were complete. Mereya's breath caught. Rain's hum sharpened into something more like a heartbeat. "My body," she said, very softly, "is in there." The crew froze on the threshold, staring into the vertical cylinder where hundreds of Kollosol's vessels slept or failed. Faber raised the rifle, scanning angles. Pippin braced Schrödinger against the rail. Merri set her hand on the wall like she could hear circuits ticking under vine.

The chamber waited.

## Chapter 26 — The Vessels of Green

The inner chamber breathed cold. Light leaked from ancient strips in the ceiling —thin, obedient, remembering how to glow. The air tasted of iron and old coolant, undercut by a wet, vegetal sweetness that didn't belong underground. The corridor behind them sealed with a hush. Before them: rows and rows of containment pods fading into a slow gray distance. Some pods stood open, glass jaws broken outward. Some were dry and dust
-filmed, their beds collapsed. But most were taken — occupied by what Kollosol had tried to make and the Kudzu had decided to keep. Bodies lay within. Not Rain —these were echoes gone wrong. Men, women, children. Limbs webbed with fibrous green. Veins turned to

capillary vines. Hair lacquered to skulls. In more than a few, the plant had grown through mouth and eyes as if the face were only a trellis. Merri's breath scraped. Even Pippin flinched before his shoulders found their iron again. Faber said nothing, the scavenger rifle snug against his shoulder, finger light on the trigger. "They weren't preserved," Mereya said. The cradle's weight pressed warm and electric against her ribs. "They were planted." Rain's voice came small and steady from the box.

"They tried to make me so many times."

A pod hissed. Sap thickened the seams. A body inside convulsed. The Kudzu poured out through it— threading joints, knotting muscles, animating meat. The puppet sat up. Its sockets glowed green. Then another. Then another. A dozen husks stepped down from their pods, patient as sleepwalkers. Their

throats swelled with sap and then pressed sound into the room — not song, but vibration. A choir made of stolen lungs. "They're singing," Merri whispered. It was pressure, not music. Enough to lever panic into the bones. Faber fired first. The coilbolt split a puppet's chest, sap hissing to vapor. It staggered, pulled itself back upright. "Spines!" he shouted. "Or heads!" Mereya's pistol barked. A husk dropped, jaw unhinging in a hiss. Pippin's hook -knife carved another low, blade slick with sap. Schrödinger fought slow but precise, each swing of his cutlass severing a tendon of Kudzu. He looked, in that moment, exactly like the Republic's legend: a man who refused subtraction. But there were too many.
The hum built and built, a dissonant tide.

Rain's voice cut through it —small, defiant. Not words. A note. The Ciliax pulsed with it. Frost etched itself across the walls in constellations. The puppets faltered, vines spasming like nerves cut with wire. Faber's shot found the pause, Mereya's pistol a gap, Pippin's knife a throat. Schrödinger barked a laugh that was mostly blood and drove his blade through another. The Kudzu adapted. The puppets screamed higher, jagged, trying to drown her out. The chamber tilted toward frenzy. "Louder," Mereya whispered. "Rain —sing louder." "I don't want to break them," Rain pleaded. "They're already broken," Faber said, and shot another spine apart. So Rain obeyed. The note lifted —pure, glass -fine. It wasn't loud. It was true. The chamber froze. Frost -lines crawled across pods and walls alike. The puppets stiffened mid step. Vines recoiled into

ceilings and vents. The pressure broke like glass under weight. Silence, except for the low hum of the pod they hadn't touched yet.

At the far wall, the vines had made something like a shrine. A single pod stood set apart, armored, immaculate, its faceplate smoky with frost. Kudzu had wreathed it but not pierced it — as though even hunger knew not to chew this door. Rain whispered, almost shy: "That one. That's me." Mereya stepped closer. Faber raised a hand. "We cut when it opens. Not before. No gaps for the plant to jam." "Understood," Pippin said, hook knife ready. Mereya pressed her palm against the glass. Warm through her glove, a warmth too human for this place. "Rain," she whispered.

"Knock like before." Rain didn't knock. She breathed. The cradle glowed, frost -lines flared, and the locks released with a sigh that sounded like relief. The

Kudzu lunged. Pippin's knife sang, Merri's cutter spat sparks, Schrödinger's blade swung low. Faber dropped a coilbolt into the heart of a vine -thick fist and burned it to rags. Mereya stood her ground, the cradle blazing against her chest, refusing to move even as a tendril coiled for her wrist. The pod lifted. Mist rolled out. Inside: a child. Small. Whole. Dark hair across her brow. Skin pale from stasis, but unspoiled. A constellation of nodes along her temple like a

map no one had finished reading. Rain's voice spoke from the cradle and from the lips of the sleeping child at once: "Is it me?" Mereya's answer broke with oath

and marrow both. "Yes."

The Kudzu didn't strike again. It stilled, vines braided tight in

rafters and walls, watching. Considering. Schrödinger shifted his cutlass and smiled a ruinous smile. "Don't," he told the green. "You've tasted enough." "Back," Faber said evenly. "We walk out." And so they did, tethered still, Rain cradled in Mereya's arms, alive and awake in the body made for her. The vines withdrew to let them pass. Not defeated. Simply patient. Outside the chamber, the cathedral swayed. The Toad did not rise. It blinked, slow as an old coin in mud, and let them go. At the Fortune's gangway, Rain turned her face against Mereya's collar and whispered, half to herself,

half to the Kudzu beyond: "I taste wrong." Rain
blinked, then looked down at herself with a small

frown. "This isn't right," she whispered. "I'm
supposed to have clothes." Faber moved to shrug out
of his coat, but Rain shook her head. "Not those. Not
borrowed. I remember." The hum rose. Threads of
light crawled across her shoulders and down her arms,
weaving themselves into
something not cloth, not armor. A dress formed —
translucent, flecked with faint stars, its hem rippling
as though cut from the night sky itself. She twirled
once, unsteady but delighted, and lifted her chin.
"Because I'm a princess." Pippin gasped, tugging
Merri's sleeve. "She looks like one." Mereya's eyes
brimmed with tears, though she smiled. Faber
lowered his coat, his gaze soft despite the hard line of
his mouth. Schrödinger muttered about gods and fairy
tales, while two of the Deceitful

Fortune crew exchanged uneasy looks —
seeing value where others saw wonder.
"Good,"
Schrödinger said, and for once, he smiled
with teeth.

End.